Christopher Columbus

Voyager to the Unknown

Christopher Columbus

Voyager to the Unknown

Nancy Smiler Levinson

LODESTAR BOOKS

DUTTON   NEW YORK

for Virginia Buckley,
with admiration and appreciation

Library of Congress Cataloging-in-Publication Data

Levinson, Nancy Smiler.
    Christopher Columbus: voyager to the unknown / by Nancy Smiler Levinson.
      p.   cm.
    "Lodestar books."
    Bibliography: p.
    Includes index.
    Summary: A biography of the fifteenth-century Italian seaman and navigator who unknowingly discovered a new continent while looking for a western route to India.
    ISBN 0-525-67292-3
    1. Columbus, Christopher—Juvenile literature.   2. Explorers—Spain—Biography—Juvenile literature.   3. Explorers—America—Biography—Juvenile literature.   4. America—Discovery and exploration—Spanish—Juvenile literature. [1. Columbus, Christopher. 2. Explorers. 3. America—Discovery and exploration—Spanish.]   I. Title.
E111.L58   1990
970.01′5—dc20   89-32254
[B]   CIP
[92]   AC

Published in the United States by Lodestar Books, an affiliate of Dutton Children's Books, a division of Penguin Books USA Inc.

Published simultaneously in Canada by Fitzhenry & Whiteside Limited, Toronto

Editor: Virginia Buckley   Designer: Richard Granald, LMD

Printed in the U.S.A.   First Edition

10 9 8 7 6 5 4 3 2 1

Contents

Author's Note   vii

Acknowledgments   ix

1 Secrets of the World   1

2 The Great Enterprise   15

3 The Dark, Mysterious Ocean   28

4 Land Ho!   34

5 Quest for Gold   39

6 Shipwrecked   49

7 Admiral of the Ocean Sea: The Second Voyage   59

8 Beginning of Bloodshed   65

9 Rebellion: The Third Voyage   71

10 The Most Dangerous Voyage   85

11 "Inventor of a New Idea"   91

12 After Columbus   97

Chronology of Events   106

Articles of Capitulation   108

Letter of Introduction   110

Crew on the First Voyage   111

Suggested Reading   114

Index   115

Author's Note

For centuries, historians and scientists have been studying and discussing Christopher Columbus and his voyages. They have also been arguing.

The reason for these arguments is that much about Columbus's background, life, and journeys is uncertain. Exactly when and where was he born? Who were his ancestors, and how far back can they be traced? Precisely at what time in his life did he decide to sail the uncharted sea? How authentic are the diaries and documents that have been found and translated? There are many other debatable questions as well.

Perhaps the most spirited debate centers around the question: Which is the exact island where Columbus landed in the Americas?

There were, of course, no maps of the New World then. They were being roughly sketched by the voyagers as they sailed and sighted islands. And the navigational directions and descriptions were being written by Columbus in his ship's diary. The voyagers did the best they could to record their whereabouts and discoveries, but accuracy was impossible. In the region where they first landed there were numerous islands. How could it be proved beyond doubt hundreds of years later that one of them (which Columbus named San Salvador) was the exact landfall site? No wonder that scholars have had a difficult puzzle to piece together.

New methods of research and the recovery of lost documents have resulted in the naming of a number of places as the landfall. For some time, scholars generally agreed that the site was Watling Island. One of the most well-known of these theorists was Samuel

Eliot Morison, a noted biographer of Columbus who retraced the route that Columbus sailed. But in 1986 a team of scientists and scholars of the National Geographic Society published new evidence to name another island, Samana Cay. This brought a loud outcry of disagreement from scholars across the globe and has added fuel to an already heated controversy. But disagreement is part of the study of history, and it is often what helps to make it so challenging.

Writing a book that involves research material translated from another language provides its own kind of challenge. Much of the material on Columbus was written in Spanish, and it is interesting to compare the wide range of translations into English. Older translations from centuries past are naturally in a formal style, since that was the custom of the time. One of the latest translations is that of the log from Columbus's ship, completed in 1987 by Robert H. Fuson, professor emeritus of geography. This is a modern, readable version. But the variant of translations also sometimes changes the meaning of the original writer's words. This too gives more cause for continued discussion.

All of this should remind us that the study of history is not necessarily a matter of definite and factual events with only one point of view. Different viewpoints and new evidence are frequently what make history exciting to scholars. As we celebrate the quincentenary of the discovery of America, the story of Columbus will again come alive for all of us.

Acknowledgments

For their assistance and continual goodwill during my research and writing of this book, I would like to thank Rebecca Magruder, friend and assistant editor, and Harriet Sigerman, production editor, at Lodestar Books; Lynne Shapiro; Fredi Chiapelli, director of Medieval and Renaissance Studies, UCLA; Geoffrey Symcox, professor of European history, UCLA; Eugene Lyon, director of the Center for Historic Research, St. Augustine Foundation; José Martinez-Hidalgo, former director of the Maritime Museum, Barcelona; Carol Urness, James Ford Bell Library, University of Minnesota; and all my patient and generous friends at the Beverly Hills Public Library.

I would also like to acknowledge Daniel J. Boorstin, Librarian Emeritus of Congress, who is the author of *The Discoverers: A History of Man's Search to Know His World and Himself,* a book of inspiration to me and a voyage in itself.

1

Secrets of the World

Long ago there was a land of people in Europe and a land of people in the Americas, before the Americas were named. But neither knew of the other's existence. It simply was impossible to know. A vast, mysterious ocean separated them—and who would dare venture across it to see what lay beyond?

It was destined, though, that one day someone with extraordinary vision and imagination would boldly set forth on such a voyage of discovery. That time arrived in the fifteenth century in Europe when the Age of Exploration had just begun.

The voyager was a man born in the ancient Italian city of Genoa in 1451. Because of sketchy records the most likely birthdate is between August 25 and the end of October. There on the seacoast as a boy he spent long hours gazing out over the ocean and watching the building of ships in the coves and harbors. As those ships came and went, trading and exploring nearby environs, he longed to follow their course and see what lay beyond his home. The boy was

1

named Christopher Columbus. And from his earliest years he yearned to know the secrets of the world.

His family was not in Genoa's important shipbuilding industry, though. Rather, his parents, Domenico and Susanna, both came from generations of wool carders and weavers. Christopher, his brothers Bartholomew and Giacomo (known in Spain as Diego), both thought to be younger, and his sister, Bianchinetta, grew up in a home of hard-working people. The family were also devout Catholics who observed holidays religiously and worshiped frequently at church. The children received no formal education, but it is likely that they attended a guild school for a while to learn the basics of arithmetic, reading, and writing.

Although Columbus's father was not a seafaring man by trade, he went to sea to sell his cloth. Columbus was about fourteen when he began accompanying his father on business excursions. These were made on small coastal vessels and always with the shoreline in sight. But at least the world began to open to the eager boy. From the earliest excursions, he took care to note the changing colors of the seas and the varying patterns of the winds and currents. Little by little, he learned how to handle the rigging, weigh anchor, steer, reef, and tack—changing course so the front of the boat passed through the eye of the wind and the sails crossed from one side to the other. He became aware of the virtues and the risks of navigation.

Columbus's city of Genoa was situated on the western coast of Italy overlooking the Ligurian Sea, which led to the Mediterranean Sea, the most important maritime trade route for the merchants of Europe. On Italy's eastern coast at the uppermost reach of the Adriatic Sea, which also led to the Mediterranean, was the city of Venice. For centuries, Genoa and Venice had engaged in bitter wars over control of the Mediterranean trade route.

A destination that rulers of both cities sought was the Christian city of Constantinople, situated on the shores of the Mediterranean and the Black Sea in the Byzantine Empire. There converged all the trade routes between Europe and the fabulous East Indies, as Asia was called. Merchants first sailed the Black Sea and then proceeded east by caravan on land. Travel was long and arduous.

Although Genoa and Venice were rivals, all of Europe prospered from this trade route. Then in 1453, when Columbus was not yet two years old, trading became difficult. The Muslim Turks from the east invaded Constantinople, conquered the city, and renamed it Istanbul. The conquerors cut off much of the trade between the east and Europe. Europe was eager to obtain gold from the east, as well as other precious stones, silks, and exotic spices such as pepper, cinnamon, ginger, and cloves. The spices were highly valued not only for enhancing the flavor of food but for masking the bad taste of tainted meat. So the opening of a direct and safe route by sea became increasingly desirable.

As Columbus was growing up, explorers were searching for such routes. The Portuguese hoped to reach the East Indies by circumnavigating Africa. But the obstacles were numerous. They had no idea how far south the continent extended or if it was circumnavigable at all. Some were convinced that the land near the equatorial torrid zone was uninhabitable. Others refused to get too close to the equator because they believed they would burn to death in the zone's "fiery waters."

Nevertheless the Portuguese pushed forward, encouraged by their king, Alfonso V. The crown was impoverished, and Alfonso hoped to pay off his debts with profits from further discoveries. Portugal already had exclusive rights to the African coast as far as it had been explored. These rights had been granted by Pope Sixtus IV in Rome. He had also granted rights to Spain for a group of islands that Spanish

No portrait painted during Columbus's lifetime appears to have survived, but many later artists rendered their own conception of the admiral. Here are three: youthful adventurer, GIOVIO MUSEUM; dignified adult, NAVAL MUSEUM OF MADRID; or thoughtful servant of the Crown, GIOVIO MUSEUM.

explorers had discovered and named the Canaries. The Pope was the supreme authority in such matters.

Columbus grew to be a well-spoken young man, tall, with light eyes and reddish-brown hair. Sailing with large commercial convoys and with whaling ships increasingly took him farther away from home, and the experience helped him to become a highly skilled mariner. He was also developing exceptional powers of observation, as he noted much about the winds, the currents, the stars, and the skies. At each new place he made notes not only on navigation and climate but described and compared the natural phenomena—animal life, fruits and flowers, and their shapes and colors and tastes. It was said that he possessed remarkable senses of sight, hearing, and smell, as well as an extraordinary intuitive sense.

One expedition he joined took him to the island of Chios, a Genoese possession in the Aegean Sea. There he stayed for many months defending from Turkish attack a business that extracted gum mastic from trees, which was used as a painkiller.

About a year after that expedition, a convoy he was on that carried a shipment of gum mastic was attacked by French pirates lying in wait. The convoy had been sailing in waters off Cape St. Vincent at the southern tip of Portugal. In the sea battle that took place many sailors were killed. Columbus jumped from a sinking ship, and was injured but spared. With the aid of a floating oar for periods of rest, he managed to swim to the Portuguese port of Lagos, a distance of six miles. After his wounds were healed, he made his way to the capital city of Lisbon, and there he decided to stay. The year was 1476. This was a turning point in Columbus's life.

Lisbon faced outward to the ocean. It looked toward the future. Although Alfonso V and his son who succeeded him, the ruthless King John II, greedily urged exploration, it was another figure who truly made Portugal the leading sea power. He was known as Prince Henry the Navigator, a nephew of Alfonso. Like Columbus, Henry felt beckoned by the unknown.

Henry was not an accomplished sailor, but he established a school for mariners where he surrounded himself with seamen, mapmakers, and cosmographers—men who studied the structure and physical features of the universe. Christians, Jews, and Muslims came from far and wide, and Henry encouraged them to study, build ships capable of making long voyages, and keep accurate logbooks and charts. By the time Columbus arrived in Portugal, Henry had died, but his sailors had discovered and named the Madeira, the Azores, and the Cape Verde islands.

The cartographers also had mapped nearly one third of Africa's length and drawn many *portolanos,* harbor guides for merchants. Trade with Africa was highly profitable. The Portuguese received pepper, elephant tusks, and chests

Prince Henry the Navigator
NATIONAL LIBRARY, PARIS

of gold dust in exchange for red caps, small, round hawk-bells that were used in falconry, Venetian beads, and horses. In addition, Portuguese caravels returned with African slaves.

Once Columbus was settled in Lisbon he joined his brother Bartholomew, who was a sailor. When not at sea, Bartholomew also ran a shop where he sold books and drew maps, for which there was a growing demand. Columbus began drawing, too, and spending time with the mariners who visited the shop. He also learned to speak Portuguese and to read and write Spanish. Strangely, in Genoa's guild school he had not learned to read and write in Italian, and Genoese was not a written language but a spoken dialect. Apparently, according to historians, the little education he received at the guild was conducted in Latin.

At the first chance, Columbus shipped out on sailing expeditions. In a short time he became familiar with Portuguese shores and learned to handle a caravel, working it toward and away from shore against the wind. He sailed down the coast of Africa, and contrary to popular belief, he concluded that land near the equator was inhabitable.

Then he ventured onto the North Atlantic Ocean, sailing to the Canary Islands, the Madeira Islands, and the Azores, learning to navigate through fog and storm and gathering clues about the ocean-wind currents. He even sailed as far north as England, Ireland, and Iceland, his first experience on the high seas. Again, he made fascinating observations, noting Iceland's extremely high tides and very short winter days at latitudes far north.

In the midst of these adventures, in his twenty-seventh year he met and married a woman named Felipa Perestrello y Moniz, daughter of a Portuguese noble family. And on the island of Porto Santo, where they lived at the beginning of their marriage, she gave birth to a son, Diego.

During these years in Portugal Columbus also began to embark on a new kind of adventure. It was an adventure of the mind and spirit. No one can say precisely when Columbus formed his grand plan or how long it took him to do so. But he became convinced that he could sail west on the uncharted ocean and reach the East Indies in about ten days' time. If he could be the one to open a shorter and safer sea route for trade, he would win riches and glory.

Most people said that the East Indies were too far away and that it would be impossible to navigate the ocean successfully. But Columbus continued to believe otherwise. First, he had gathered a great deal of experience at sea. Then, too, he heard a number of tales told by mariners who swore them to be true. One told of a sea pilot finding a carved piece of wood adrift hundreds of miles west of Cape St. Vincent. Another claimed that on an island in the Azores the sea had flung ashore two dead bodies with faces quite different from the Christians of Europe. Certainly then, Columbus thought, these East Indies could not be far off.

Another important consideration centered around the ideas and beliefs Columbus had formed about the size of the world. Of course, educated people understood that the earth was round, and many cartographers, although never having circumnavigated the earth, drew maps and charts according to their calculations. Columbus and Bartholomew studied them at length. Columbus also spent much time reading works by the ancient scholars and talking to astronomers and cosmographers.

For centuries men had been trying to find their place on the earth as well as in time. But with limited knowledge they had to depend on their observations of the stars, the moon, and lunar eclipses. Ancient Greeks and Egyptians had determined that the earth was a sphere. An astronomer named Hipparchus had not only calculated a round earth, but even thought of dividing it with lines on the surface. These signified the globe's latitude (imaginary east-west parallel lines around the globe that indicate location north or south of the equator) and longitude (imaginary north-south lines from the two poles indicating location east or west of the prime meridian, which is a great reference circle around the surface of the earth, passing through the two poles). Both latitude and longitude came to be measured in degrees.

When Columbus began to read the writings of the ancient scholars, he paid particular attention to the astronomer and geographer Ptolemy. Among Ptolemy's many theories about the universe was the belief that it was possible to explore, but it was unthinkable to travel infinitely with no limits. Although this was not helpful to Columbus, another theory was. In estimating the size of the earth, Ptolemy figured it to be half its actual size. To

The Martin Behaim globe, the first known of its kind, was constructed in 1492, the same year that Columbus discovered America. Behaim's ideas of the world were similar to those of Columbus. It is uncertain whether or not Columbus and Behaim ever met. GERMAN NATIONAL MUSEUM

Columbus, this meant the distance by ocean from Europe to Asia was shorter than his contemporaries believed. This encouraged him, and so did the ideas of a second-century Greek mathematical geographer named Marinus of Tyre, who also estimated more land surface. Columbus was inspired too by the biblical prophet Esdras, who figured that the Indies extended far eastward because as he saw it, the earth consisted of six parts land and only one part water. This was a popular notion in medieval times.

As Columbus read, he underlined ideas that he agreed with and scribbled notes in the margins of his books. In a world geography book, *Imago mundi,* by Cardinal Pierre d'Ailly, Columbus wrote, "The end of Spain and the beginning of India are not far distant but close, and it is evident that this sea is navigable in a few days with a fair wind." The ancient geographer Strabo had fixed the earth's circumference at 18,000 miles, but Columbus determined it to be

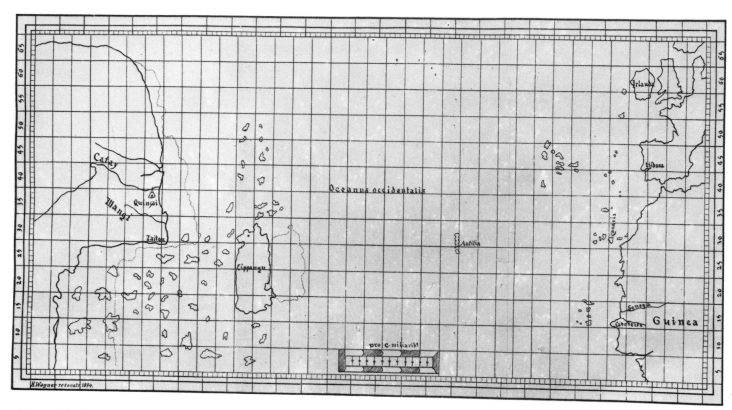

Toscanelli's chart, showing no continent between Europe and the East Indies NATIONAL LIBRARY OF AUSTRIA, VIENNA

closer to 20,000 and measured 56 miles to each degree of the 360 degrees longitude. (The actual circumference is 25,000 miles, and there are 69 miles to a longitudinal degree.)

Further encouragement came from a cosmographer, Paolo dal Pozzo Toscanelli, known as Paul the Physician. As the story goes (a few historians question the authenticity of the letters between Toscanelli and Columbus), Columbus heard that Toscanelli had drawn a chart that greatly underestimated the width of the ocean. He wrote to Toscanelli at his home in Florence, Italy, and Toscanelli replied, "I perceive your noble and grand desire to go to the places where the spices grow." The voyage was not only possible, he said, but "honorable . . . and most glorious among all Christians." Included was a copy of his hand-drawn chart. An acquaintance of Columbus's, Bishop Bartholomew de las

Casas, said Toscanelli's map "set Christopher Columbus's mind ablaze."

With the passing of months, Columbus also began to feel destined by God to go forth on his journey. After all, he was named after Saint Christopher, the Bearer of Christ, and did that not make him a messenger of God?

Image of St. Christopher, bearing Christ on his back
NAVAL MUSEUM OF MADRID

11

As for what Columbus expected to find in the East Indies, it had been described two hundred years earlier in a volume called *The Book of Marco Polo.* Marco Polo, one of the world's most remarkable travelers, left an astonishing set of stories about the Asian continent—its geography and climate, its customs, politics, and religion. He told of rubies, pearls, and sapphires, and gold and silver mines. He wrote of the places where all the spices grow and how he watched silk spun from worms, a deeply guarded Chinese secret. He described monkeys, elephants, rhinoceroses, and other living creatures never seen by a European. One such creature was a monstrous-jawed serpent beast "so horrible that no man can approach them without terror." These were crocodiles.

Marco Polo was born in Venice in 1254. When he was seventeen he joined his merchant father and uncle on a bold and dangerous adventure. From Italy they sailed the Adriatic and Mediterranean seas, then journeyed with pack animals overland through Arabia and sailed again on the Persian Gulf. Their caravan continued on foot 3,000 miles across the Gobi Desert through intense heat and dust storms to Cathay, which is now China. It took three and a half years to reach their destination—the dominion of the Kublai Khan, ruler of the vast Chinese Empire, which had been conquered by his grandfather, Genghis Khan.

The Grand Khan graciously received the travelers at his gilded summer palace, which was walled in a sixteen-mile area that included meadows, groves, and hunting grounds stocked with deer, horses, and elephants. Ten thousand servants and guards attended the Khan there and at his palace in Peking, the capital. In short time he became so fond of Marco Polo that he took him into his service too, even though he was a foreigner. Marco Polo conducted official business and traveled widely for the Khan. There

Marco Polo sets sail from Venice. BODLEIAN LIBRARY, OXFORD, ENGLAND

was one problem, however. The Polos were not allowed to leave, and so they stayed for seventeen years.

Finally they were asked to accompany a bride-to-be on her journey to marry a Persian ruler. With a fleet of fourteen ships they sailed the South China Sea and traveled over the Indian Ocean, rounding India and then going northward on the Arabian Sea to Persia, now Iran. By the time they reached the city of Hormuz, nearly two years had

13

passed and 600 people had died along the way. The bride-to-be survived, but the groom was no longer alive. Marco Polo and his aging father and uncle had no intention of returning to Cathay, so they left the girl with the son of the deceased ruler, who married her himself.

The three travelers then set out for Italy by way of Persia, the Black Sea to Constantinople, and the Mediterranean. Upon reaching home, they had to convince their family that they were, indeed, still alive, and to convince Venice that the tales they told were true.

Meanwhile, Venice and Genoa were at war again, and a year after his return Marco Polo was captured and imprisoned by the Genoese. To pass the time, he told his stories to his prison mates. One fellow, known only by the name of Rustichello, thought the stories were so wondrous that he had Marco Polo dictate them to him. The result was the book later copied by scribes in different languages and printed some years after the invention of the printing press in 1450. This book sparked the imaginations of all Europeans, especially explorers.

One explorer who read the book many times was Christopher Columbus. With unshakable conviction, by 1484 he began devoting all his time and energy to his plan to seek a western and shorter route to the East Indies. He called it the Enterprise of the Indies.

2

The Great Enterprise

Columbus could not carry out his plan alone, of course. He needed cooperation and financial backing. The first person he went to was the King of Portugal, John II. King John listened attentively, but that was all. The disappointed Columbus felt that the "Lord closed King John's eyes and ears, for I failed to make him understand what I was saying." King John did understand, however, and played a dirty trick on Columbus. He sent a secret mission of caravels, hoping his own men would make the discovery for him and thereby avoid having to reward the foreigner. But the crew lacked knowledge and skills on the high seas, and after being thrashed about in a storm they were forced to return.

Columbus was furious when he found out. He had other problems as well. For one, his wife, Felipa, died around that time. For another, since he did not have steady work, he found himself in debt. So he and his five-year-old son, Diego, left Portugal for the port of Palos in Spain. From the port they walked three and a half miles to a Franciscan

King John II of Portugal
HISTORICAL MUSEUM, VIENNA

monastery at La Rábida. Kindhearted monks, Friars Juan Pérez and Antonio Marchena, welcomed Columbus and encouraged his plan. They also took in Diego, who remained at the monastery to receive an education.

Now Columbus turned to the Spanish crown for help. But it was clear from the start that his mission would not be an easy one. First, he needed an introduction to the king and queen. Then it was a matter of traveling to the court, which was held at the time in the city of Córdoba. The court never stayed in the same locale. Medieval courts spent money lavishly, and as soon as they had used up the money

16

and resources of one city, they moved to another. Friar Pérez paved the way for the introduction at Córdoba, but the first meeting did not take place for a long time.

King Ferdinand and Queen Isabella had other matters on their minds. They were the Catholic sovereigns, given the title by Pope Alexander VI, and they were occupied with trying to unify Spain into a Catholic country. Their mission required them to rid the land of all Jews and Moors.

Spain had long been forcing Jews to convert to Catholicism, which, during that time, was the only form of Chris-

La Rábida as it appears today
PROVINCIAL FOUNDATION OF
TOURISM, HUELVA, SPAIN

King Ferdinand BY
PERMISSION OF HER MAJESTY
THE QUEEN ELIZABETH II.
ROYAL COLLECTION, ST.
JAMES'S PALACE, LONDON

Queen Isabella BY PERMISSION
OF HER MAJESTY THE QUEEN
ELIZABETH II. ROYAL
COLLECTION, ST. JAMES'S
PALACE, LONDON

tianity. When this failed to work completely, the sovereigns and the Pope established the Spanish Inquisition. That brutal institution caused thousands of Jews to be tortured and burned at the stake and thousands more to be driven out of the land to other European countries and Africa. Much of their money and belongings were confiscated and used to wage war on the Moors, who held a stronghold at the southern tip of Spain in Granada. The Catholic sovereigns used Spain's money not only to finance the war but to increase shipping and strengthen their naval forces. So they were in no position to help Columbus with financing. It was a year before they even received him.

Ferdinand was a cold and cunning king who paid little attention to the foreigner. In contrast, the high-minded and earnest Isabella was the same age as Columbus and seemed to get along with him quite well. At least she listened and encouraged his dreams. But the best she could do was offer him a small amount of money to live on for a while. He had no choice but to wait. Meanwhile he sent his brother Bartholomew to England with his plan, hoping that Henry VII would be interested enough to finance the voyage. Bartholomew was captured by pirates, however, and did not come back until years later.

The banner of the Spanish Inquisition NATIONAL LIBRARY OF AUSTRIA, VIENNA

During his wait Columbus met a woman named Beatrice Enriquez de Arana, who in 1488 gave birth to his second son, Ferdinand. That same year, news arrived that the Portuguese explorer Bartholomew Dias had rounded the Cape of Good Hope at the southern tip of Africa. This meant that a new sea route had been discovered, and unfortunately for Columbus it made his voyage less urgent.

When Columbus was granted a second audience at court two years earlier, it was only with Isabella. He promised her that his conquest would bring glory to Spain and spread

Christianity across the ocean. He was so successful in arousing her interest that she not only advanced him more money but appointed a commission to study his plan. The council, which met at Salamanca University, was presided over by Isabella's priest confessor, Friar Hernando de Talavera, and became known as the Talavera Commission. The members were important men of learning.

During the time when the Age of Exploration was beginning, a revival of art and culture flourished in Europe. This was called the Renaissance. It had begun in Italy and was growing in influence throughout Europe. The Renaissance was marked by a new spirit and interest in man—his artistic expression, education, religion and morals. Michelangelo and Leonardo da Vinci were great artists who both lived during Columbus's time.

No doubt, many members of the Talavera Commission were influenced by the burgeoning Renaissance and were becoming more open-minded in their views of humanity and the universe. But some still believed in medieval myths and witchcraft. Their arguments against Columbus's plan were numerous: Even if the width of the ocean was known, it was most likely unnavigable. No one could say for certain if there were land on the other side or if such a faraway place could be inhabited. To leave the hemisphere would mean going downhill, and therefore, it would be impossible to return. And so the arguments went.

In short, the learned men concluded the foreigner was quite mad, and they declared the enterprise vain and impossible. This judgment took four and a half years.

Meanwhile, six years had passed since Columbus had arrived in Spain. Understandably, he grew more bitter and anguished, but he was stubborn and determined. And so he stayed. Finally Isabella sent for him again. The court had moved to Santa Fé, in the region of Granada. Considerable gains were being made in conquering the Moors.

Another commission was convened for further review. This became the Royal Council of Castile, and it did not reject the enterprise. But it opposed Columbus's demands for reward. He wanted the titles Admiral of the Ocean Sea and Governor and Viceroy of all lands he might discover. Moreover, those titles should be passed on to his sons. In addition, both he and his heirs should receive a commission of 10 percent of all commerce, including gold, silver, and all other precious gems and spices. The council and Isabella found these demands absurd and dismissed Columbus.

Several months later, in January of 1492, the long and costly war between Spain and the Moors ended, and Granada fell to Spain. Columbus's hopes rose once more. However, his optimism was short-lived, because the court delivered him a final refusal and a message of farewell. Deeply embittered, Columbus saddled his mule and left. All that time wasted! Now he would have to go to France and start over.

But suddenly everything was not lost after all. As Columbus set out on the road, the chief tax collector and financial adviser to the king, Luis de Santángel, approached the queen. He had met Columbus four years earlier and believed in him. A few other diplomats supported Columbus too. Santángel offered to loan a large sum toward the enterprise. At that moment Isabella found it in her heart and mind to accept Santángel's help and to send Christopher Columbus on his voyage in the name of Catholic Spain. She quickly dispatched a messenger to catch up with him. The messenger found him four miles away, and there on the bridge at Pinos, Columbus received the news that at last he would have his Enterprise of the Indies.

On April 17, 1492, King Ferdinand and Queen Isabella signed a document that came to be known as the Articles of Capitulations. They also wrote a passport and a letter of introduction to the foreign rulers whom Columbus would meet. Since they didn't know the names of the Grand Khan or the other rulers, they left a blank space for Columbus to fill in.

Orders included the expedition to be outfitted at Palos, a small town with a good harbor. The royal decree demanded that the town provide three fully rigged vessels. Preparation costs amounted to two million *maravedis,* which came from loans provided by Santángel, the townspeople of Palos, and a number of other patrons. In addition, Columbus invested money borrowed from Genoa's banks, including Banco di San Giorgio, the Genoese state bank.

The royal order was followed, and work began on outfitting the three vessels. They were not all called ships, though. The term ship, or *nao,* was reserved for the flagship, the *Santa María,* a larger and stronger sailing craft than the other two, the *Niña* and the *Pinta,* which were known as caravels. Caravels were smaller, lighter, swifter, and considerably more manageable for exploring coasts and islands.

Even though the *Santa María* was larger than the caravels, still she was not very large. The forty men and boys who were to be accommodated on the ship were going to be cramped and crowded. They were going to have to sleep in shifts and fight for sleeping space on deck. Precise measurements were never written down, or perhaps they were not preserved, but the ship was about seventy-eight feet long. Columbus and all seamen of the day used ancient methods of measurement. They estimated tonnage cargo capacity by the number of wine barrels, or "tuns," that a ship could carry. Historians have fixed the *Santa María*'s capacity at a little over 100 tonnage.

All three vessels came to be known by names other than their original ones because ships and caravels were first named after a saint but usually nicknamed after the ship-

23

Model of the nao, *or Santa María, under the plan and directions of Captain José Martinez-Hidalgo, 1963*
MARITIME MUSEUM OF BARCELONA

owner or town where they were built. The *Santa María* was first called *La Gallega,* and the *Niña* first called *Santa Clara.* The *Pinta*'s original name remains unknown.

Columbus was to command the flagship, the *Santa María.* A mariner named Vicente Yañez Pinzón was to command the *Niña,* while his brother, Martín Alonso Pinzón, an able sailor but a temperamental man, was to command the *Pinta.* From their first meeting in Palos, Columbus and Martín

24

Pinzón harbored suspicions and ill thoughts toward each other.

The Pinzón brothers were trusted citizens and sailors of the Palos region, and after they agreed to join the expedition as officers, crew members began to sign on. A curious mixture of men would make the journey. Among them were able seamen, a surgeon, carpenters, a silversmith, a language interpreter, servants to the royal crown, the owner and master of the *Santa María,* Juan de la Cosa, and several

Vicente Yañez Pinzón, captain of the Niña *(left)* NAVAL MUSEUM OF MADRID

Martín Alonso Pinzón, captain of the Pinta *(right)* NAVAL MUSEUM OF MADRID

Ferdinand and Isabella see Columbus off from the dock at Palos. LIBRARY OF CONGRESS

boys who had never been to sea. There were also four criminals who had been pardoned by the Spanish court in order to join the crew. One had been condemned to death for killing a man, and the other three had committed a crime by helping him escape. The *Niña* carried twenty-four men, and the *Pinta,* twenty-six. Of the ninety men total on all three vessels, all were Spanish, except for one Portuguese mariner and three Italians, including Christopher Columbus himself.

The recruiting and outfitting took three months, and departure was set for August 3. That date was important in Spanish history for another reason as well. The Inquisition had ordered all remaining Jews expelled from the Spanish Empire by the end of July. At the last minute, the final departure date had been extended three days. So while Columbus's expedition set out to expand the world, in the harbor they passed the ships that carried Spain's last Jews, weeping, from their homes.

The sailors took communion at church, and the fleet embarked at dawn. On August 3, 1492, Columbus began a journal (the original journal, which ended March 15, 1493, disappeared, but copies were made, although some parts were paraphrased, omitted, or rewritten). That day he wrote that they departed from the Palos harbor of Saltés and "traveled with a strong breeze . . . making for the Canaries." The most momentous voyage in history had begun.

3

The Dark,
Mysterious Ocean

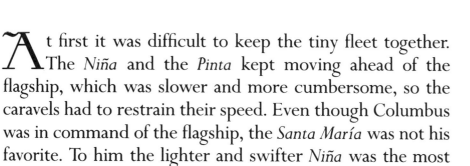

At first it was difficult to keep the tiny fleet together. The *Niña* and the *Pinta* kept moving ahead of the flagship, which was slower and more cumbersome, so the caravels had to restrain their speed. Even though Columbus was in command of the flagship, the *Santa María* was not his favorite. To him the lighter and swifter *Niña* was the most seaworthy.

The vessels set their course south by west as they headed toward the Canary Islands. For the most part, Spain had conquered and claimed these islands, which were 800 miles away. Columbus considered them a good place to stop to secure fresh provisions of meat, cheese, water, and wood.

In short time it became necessary to stop for repairs as well. On August 6, the *Pinta* signaled news of trouble by sending up smoke in an iron vessel used for burning charcoal. Her rudder had worked its way loose from its mounting. Three days later she reached one of the islands, the

Model of the caravel Niña, *built under the direction of Captain Enrico D'Albertis in 1892* CIVIC NAVAL MUSEUM OF GENOA AT PEGLI

Model of the caravel Pinta, *built under the direction of Captain Enrico D'Albertis in 1892* CIVIC NAVAL MUSEUM OF GENOA AT PEGLI

Grand Canary, and stopped there to have the rudder re-attached. Contrary winds prevented the other vessels from reaching that island, so they went on to Gomera, one of the other Canary Islands, where they arrived several days later. There, in addition to gathering provisions, they replaced the triangular lateen sails on the *Niña* with *redonda,* square sails, which could withstand strong winds on the high seas better. After that they made for the Grand Canary.

The rudder repairs on the *Pinta* were not satisfactory, so Columbus decided that a new rudder had to be built. This delay caused the three vessels to remain longer than

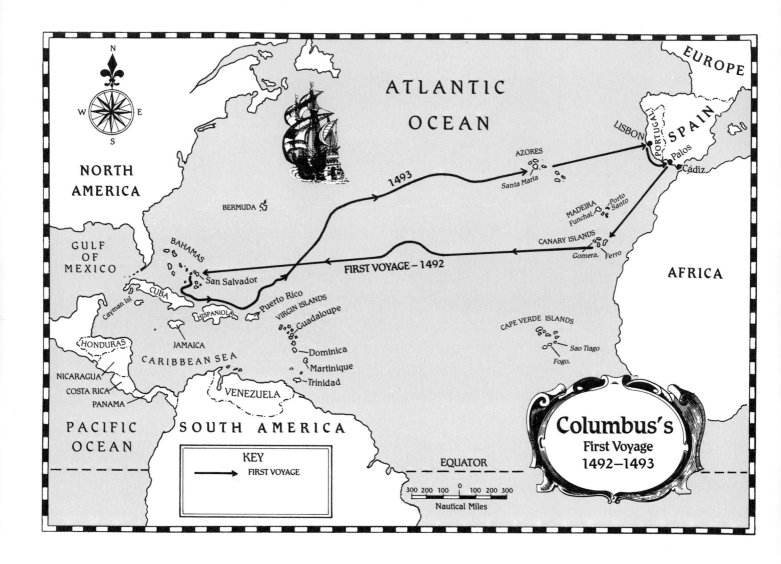

ATLANTIC OCEAN

NORTH AMERICA

1493

BERMUDA

GULF OF MEXICO

BAHAMAS

San Salvador

CUBA

Cayman Isl.

HISPANIOLA

Puerto Rico

VIRGIN ISLANDS

Guadaloupe

JAMAICA

CARIBBEAN SEA

Dominica

Martinique

Trinidad

HONDURAS

NICARAGUA

COSTA RICA

PANAMA

PACIFIC OCEAN

SOUTH AMERICA

VENEZUELA

EUROPE

LISBON

PORTUGAL

SPAIN

Palos

Cádiz

AZORES

Santa María

MADEIRA

Funchal

Porto Santo

CANARY ISLANDS

Gomera, Ferro

AFRICA

FIRST VOYAGE – 1492

CAPE VERDE ISLANDS

Sao Tiago

Fogo

KEY

FIRST VOYAGE

EQUATOR

300 200 100 0 100 200 300

Nautical Miles

Columbus's First Voyage 1492–1493

planned, and it was not until September 9 that they finally hoisted sails and departed. The course was set due west, as they headed directly for the island kingdom of Japan (called Cipangu), which according to Columbus's calculations was on the same latitude as the Canaries. Beyond Japan, then, Columbus expected to reach the Asian mainland at China.

It was dusk when they set sail out of the Canaries over calm waters. But the seamen on board were hardly calm. This time as they moved away from land, it seemed to them that the world was disappearing. They were beginning to feel alone and frightened. Finally by nightfall, all sight of land had disappeared. A dark, mysterious, uncharted ocean now stretched before the men. They did not know how long the voyage would take, or where they would arrive, or if they would even return home.

Columbus, however, was full of optimism. To him everything looked certain and hopeful. Even the winds that were carrying them westward were glorious. These were the trade winds, always blowing in the same direction from east to west. They were constant and fair and kept the ship on the same latitude as the Canary Islands without blowing them off course.

While Columbus was optimistic, he understood the men's fears. So he decided that in addition to his daily journal, he would keep a second account of the distance the vessels traveled. The first account would be the accurate one, which he would keep privately. The other he "determined to count less than the true number so that the crew might not be dismayed if the voyage should prove long." A sea league is a unit of measurement that is about 2.82 nautical miles, although Columbus used a slightly different number that figured closer to 3.18 nautical miles to a sea league. On September 10 he noted privately that they had made 20 leagues that day. In the false journal he "reckoned only 16."

Actually no mariner at that time could accurately determine the speed of a ship. For orienting themselves, mariners had the compass, called a magnetic needle, which was a mystical instrument because it always pointed toward the North Star (Polaris). But little was known then about the pull exerted on the compass by the earth's magnetic field. Beyond the compass they were left to their own sightings and judgment at sea. It was far from scientific and not at all easy. The most common method for estimating distance was "dead reckoning"—plotting the course and position by direction, time, and speed. This meant guessing speed

Sighting the sun with a cross-staff, a crude navigational device used after Columbus NEW YORK PUBLIC LIBRARY

from a fixed point by watching an object such as a star or a piece of seaweed. In addition to the compass and dead reckoning, Columbus also navigated by soundings, which he did by lowering a tallow-covered lead weight to the sea floor to estimate depth.

For the first week out from the Canary Islands, the fleet continued to sail due west in fair weather. Columbus wrote that the "mornings were a source of great delight for all and lacked nothing to make them more enchanting, except perhaps a song of nightingales."

The sailors, bearded (except for Columbus), barefoot, and dressed in short, gray, blouselike garments and red woolen stocking caps, quickly fell into routine. They were divided into two watches of four hours each. The periods for standing watch and for sleeping were marked by the half-hour sandglass called an *ampoletta*. It was the duty of the gromets, the ships' boys, to watch all the sand filter to the bottom and then turn the glass immediately. The glass was fragile and could break easily, so many were brought along.

There was no fear of immediate hunger because there were enough stores on board to last a year. The vessels carried wine, water, salt meat and barreled salt sardines and anchovies, cheese, chick peas, lentils, beans, rice, oil, vinegar, garlic, honey, almonds, and raisins. Stowed in the driest parts were sea biscuits called hard tack, a type of bread that was baked ashore with wheat flour. The men had one hot meal a day, and they ate from wooden bowls with their fingers.

Columbus and his men were devoted Christians, sailing under the flags of the Catholic sovereigns, Queen Isabella and King Ferdinand of Spain. Every morning they faithfully recited prayers, and every evening they gathered together and sang "Salve Regina," an ancient hymn of praise to Mary, the Queen of Heaven. On a journey like this, they took comfort in knowing that God was watching over them.

So routine had ship life become after one week that some of the seamen began to show signs of boredom. But that was not to be for long. On September 16, when they were more than a thousand miles from the Canaries, events changed, and there were whispers of mutiny against the commander of the fleet.

Land Ho!

Suddenly the men found the sea covered with a thick, floating weed. With every mile it grew thicker until finally the entire surface of the ocean appeared a yellowish green, the color of the weed. The men were greatly alarmed. Perhaps they had gone too far in tempting fate. Now they feared being stuck at sea.

As if that weren't enough, they lost the trade winds, which was puzzling and also fearful, for they wondered if there would be any winds capable of carrying them back to Spain. Some of the men began to grumble and whisper. What if they were to heave Columbus overboard? Then they could turn back, if it was not already too late. And if they made it safely, they could tell the king and queen that Columbus accidentally fell into the ocean while observing the stars.

Columbus was well aware of these grumblings. But he managed to reassure the men of westerly winds for the return voyage. He also showed them his false distance chart to make them believe they weren't as far from home as they thought. Furthermore, he convinced them they would not be trapped by the weed. Indeed, the weed did not prevent the fleet from moving forward.

A keen observer of nature, Columbus closely studied the weed. He noted in his journal that the plants were constantly growing fresh green sprouts at one end, while at the other end air-filled, berrylike globules kept the weed afloat.

Of course, it was not known then that the fleet had entered the Sargasso Sea in the midst of the North Atlantic Ocean, and that the gulfweed came from algae plants originating in prehistoric times.

The trade winds did not pick up again for a while, so the fleet sailed slowly after that. The men remained suspicious, but toward the end of September they were given new hope. Tropical birds were sighted. This meant they could not be far from land. Then, on September 25, Martín Pinzón shouted with joy over to the *Santa María* that he sighted land. Everyone fell to his knees to give thanks to the Lord. But, to their disappointment, after sailing for another day, they came upon no land. It was a false landfall.

By early October the men were becoming more disgruntled than ever. They had been at sea without sight of land nearly four weeks now, and they were beginning to feel doomed. Again Columbus tried to be reassuring, reminding them of the promised rewards from the fabulous Indies. But it was becoming more and more difficult to calm the sailors. Finally, on October 6 the commanders conferred on what should be done. A yawl, a small servicing boat, was lowered from the *Santa María* into the ocean to pick up the Pinzón brothers and bring them aboard. They both reported that most of their men wanted to turn back. Martín Pinzón, himself, was undecided, but Columbus refused.

The following morning there was another false landfall, which was prompted by what turned out to be only a squall of clouds seen in the distance. But afterward, Columbus gave in to Martín Pinzón's plea to alter the course to southwest by west in order to follow a flock of birds that had flown overhead at the time of the last false landfall. They continued to follow that course for two more days, October 8 and 9. The next day, October 10, was the most crucial day of the voyage. The men lost all patience. On the *Santa María* there were continual rumblings of open revolt.

Of course they had long passed the position where Columbus predicted that Japan lay, but he could not give up now. This was the mission of his life, and he felt he was chosen by God to carry it forth. He had given up everything, waiting seven years for King Ferdinand and Queen Isabella to finance the voyage and send him with their blessings. And before that he had spent considerable time in Portugal preparing his ideas for this grand plan. At nearly every turn during those years, it seemed, he met with people who believed that his ideas and plan were folly. But he was sure he was right, and he needed to prove it.

Once more he tried persuading the men to allow him to complete his mission. He told them it was useless to complain since they had come so far, and that with the help of the Lord, he would find the Indies. So certain was he that he made them a promise. If they did not meet with success within two or three days, he said, he gave his word that they would turn back. Torn between fear and hope, the seamen agreed.

At the fleet's departure from Spain, the king and queen had promised a reward to the first man who sighted land— ten thousand *maravedis* every year for life. A *maravedi* was worth about seven-tenths of a cent in gold, so the reward meant $700 in gold, a considerable amount for a seaman whose wages on the voyage were only a thousand *maravedis* a month. All hands on deck were busy, but every man was alert, eager to be the one to fire the signal for land. The sailors on the *Pinta* were in the best position for doing so, since the *Pinta* led the fleet that day, October 10.

By the next morning no more complaints were heard. The air was filled with anticipation. A thorn with roseberries on it was found in the water. As the day passed, the *Niña* picked up a green branch with a flower on it, the *Pinta* found a cane or a stick that looked as if it had been carved, and a reed floated past the *Santa María*. Spirits were high.

At sunset a breeze turned into gale force, carrying the vessels along at considerable speed. The clouds were swept away, leaving a clear horizon. Soon afterward a bright quarter moon shone above. About 10 P.M. after the seamen had sung the "Salve Regina," the *Santa María* lay about thirty-five miles offshore. Standing on the forecastle deck at the bow of the ship, Columbus believed he saw a light, "like a little wax candle whose flame went up and down." Immediately he called Pedro Gutiérrez, a servant of King Ferdinand, who agreed that he too had seen such a light. But Rodrigo Sánchez, a comptroller sent by the king, said he saw nothing.

Then, at last, at 2 A.M. on October 12 a great cry went up. "Land ho! Land ho!" A bombard was fired into the air. This time it really was land! The men wept for joy. They prayed and sang. As Christopher Columbus had told them, it was destiny.

The sailor who had shouted and fired the signal was a man on the *Pinta* named Rodrigo de Triana, but unfortunately he was never able to collect the reward. Columbus later insisted the flickering light he saw was actually the first sighting of land, and it was he who took the promised *maravedis*. Some historians speculate that the light was the glow of torchwood used by Indians to fish by night or to ward off sand fleas, and others guess it was Columbus's imagination.

Whether he saw a light or not, it is hard to believe that the man who had conceived this extraordinary plan and voyage of discovery would allow someone else to take credit for being the first to sight land. Clearly, he felt the honor belonged to him.

The fleet could not proceed directly to the strip of beach that lay before them. The winds were too strong, and in the darkness there was too much chance of running into shoals or rocks near shore. Columbus wisely decided to drop anchor and wait until dawn. The men slept little during the wait. They were too excited and full of anticipation. Some say that night on the *Niña,* the *Pinta,* and the *Santa María* was the most momentous night on board any ships in history.

5

Quest for Gold

At last, day broke on Friday, October 12, 1492, and the fleet weighed anchor and made for land. As they approached, they saw a deserted sandy beach stretched ahead of them, but rough winds and waters prevented them from landing just then. So they circled westward, and finally toward noon found a small sheltered bay. There they anchored and set down the launches, armed with small weaponry, so that Columbus and the other officers could row ashore.

The moment they set foot on land, they fell to their knees, kissed the earth, and gave thanks to the Lord. Exultant with pride, the great visionary explorer stepped forward and displayed the fleet's royal banners with the holy cross. The name he chose for the island was San Salvador (Holy Savior), although the native name, as he later learned, was Guanahaní. Then with the secretary, Rodrigo de Escobedo, and the paymaster, Rodrigo Sánchez, as official witnesses, Columbus declared possession of the island in the name of the king and queen of Spain.

A 1493 engraving showing Columbus landing in the New World NATIONAL LIBRARY OF AUSTRIA, VIENNA

All the while this ceremony was taking place, native islanders were hiding behind trees, watching. They were people with skin of copper color who had never seen white men before, and they believed that these mysterious visitors suddenly appeared from heaven. Columbus, of course, was certain he had landed in the East Indies on an island off the Asian mainland. That is how the natives came to be called Indians.

Although Columbus thought that he had reached the East Indies, he had actually landed on the Bahama Islands, part of what is today called the West Indies. The exact island of the landfall has been a subject of argument ever since, and in all, nine places have been named. Until recently, most historians have agreed that it was the place later known as Watling Island. In 1986, however, a team of various scientists and scholars of the National Geographic Society in Washington, D.C., declared the historic landfall to be Samana Cay, an island sixty-five miles southeast of Watling. Their theory was published by team members Joseph Judge, Luis Marden, and Eugene Lyon.

Samana Cay was first named as the landfall in 1882 by Gustavus V. Fox, Abraham Lincoln's assistant secretary of the navy. The National Geographic Society team confirmed this landfall after five years of research. This included the study of a new translation of Columbus's log by Eugene Lyon, director of the Center for Historic Research, St. Augustine Foundation. Then a "track," a route, was drawn across the ocean based on the directions from that translation, while also allowing for variables in winds and currents. Finally the geography of the Bahamas was digitized, and an electronic computer was used to trace suggested routes.

Whatever the site actually was, it is agreed that the event marked the first meeting of the old world and the new, which changed the story of humankind on earth forever. The natives of the new world were once Siberian hunters, who came to the Americas during the Ice Age some 25,000 years earlier as they followed the herds southward. For the most part, Columbus encountered a people who were gentle and peaceful. They dwelled in thatched huts and had few possessions. They lived on vegetables they grew and the cassava bread they baked.

Columbus was startled to find people "quite naked as their mothers bore them." He described them as young and handsome, with hair coarse as a horse's tail, noting that many men painted their faces and bodies. "They bear no arms, nor know thereof," he wrote, "for I showed them swords and they grasped them by the blade and cut themselves through ignorance." After further describing them as

Indians navigated on rafts.
NEW YORK PUBLIC LIBRARY

simple, defenseless souls, seemingly without religion, Columbus observed they "ought to be good servants and of good skill . . . and would easily be made Christians."

The letter of introduction was of no use here. Neither was the translator, Luis de Torres. As a converted Jew, he spoke Hebrew, but Columbus had brought him along because he knew the Arabic tongue, which was believed to be spoken by the Grand Khan. The Christians from Europe and the Indians turned to hand gestures for communication. To win the Indians' trust, Columbus presented them with small trinkets such as glass beads, red caps, glass mirrors, and hawkbells, which were round bronze bells used in falconry. These gifts of little value delighted the native people. In exchange they presented the "men from the sky" with parrots, skeins of woven cloth, and even bits of broken pottery.

It was apparent that there was no abundance of gold here, and after spending the first night back on ship, the crew hoisted the sails the next day to begin exploring. Columbus was eager to find "the place where gold is born." He concluded it was Cipangu, today's Japan, which he figured must be nearby. According to the route Marco Polo had described, Columbus planned to sail south and then west. He also planned to take some Indians along as guides, and this he did by force. Columbus's quest had begun.

There appeared to be so many islands it was difficult to know where they should head first. They decided on the largest, and Columbus named it Santa María de la Concepción (now Crooked Island) after the patroness of Christians. He soon learned, though, that there was no treasure to be found there, but his captives indicated that bracelets for the arms, legs, ears, and noses could be found farther along. Columbus took this to be a good sign and set sail at once, anchoring at another island, which he named Fernandina, for King Ferdinand (now Long Island).

This was an island that abounded in beauty, and Columbus made notes about its trees and meadows, mountains and hills, and the sweet song of its nightingale. He also noted that because there was no river or stream, fresh water was highly valuable, and the natives had to collect drinking water from the rain. The natives, much like the ones on San Salvador, lived in a cluster of huts in their village and slept on long, woven nets tied at either end, which then swung suspended on poles. The Indians called them *hamacas,* which became known as hammocks. The Spaniards adopted this idea and later used hammocks on their sailing vessels.

But this enchanting place did not yield treasures either. Yet there were indications they were getting closer. One native man wore a gold nose ring with markings inscribed on it. Columbus believed they were Chinese or Japanese

43

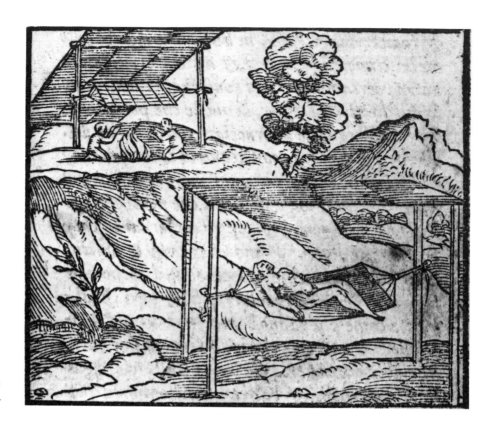

Indians sleeping on hammocks
NEW YORK PUBLIC LIBRARY

letters, so when the crew departed after heavy rains—
which had held them back—he was full of hope. One week
from the day of their landfall had passed.

Columbus decided that the fleet should separate and fan
out in the continued search, and he instructed that the first
vessel to sight land should signal by gunfire. Early the next
morning the *Pinta* fired the signal, and fresh northerly
winds helped all to converge onto an island that Columbus
named for the queen, Isabela. (It retained the Spanish
spelling. It is now Fortune Island.) Here there was a great
variety of trees, flocks of parrots and other tropical birds,
and a delicious fragrance in the air. As happened now on
island after island, the natives gladly accepted the gifts
offered to them, and in turn were eager to please the men
from the sky. To do so they always gestured about somewhere else whenever they were questioned about gold.

Columbus wanted to believe he was on the right course, so he made certain that he found clues to prove this. This time the Indians gestured toward nearby land they called Colba, and another region they called Bohío. Instead of Colba, Columbus heard the name Cipangu and convinced himself that he was near Japan. Colba was actually today's Cuba, and Bohío (the Indian word for house) was the present-day island of Haiti and the Dominican Republic.

Cuba was a three-day journey south in fair winds. Once more the fleet found natural beauty and a few curious Indian fishermen, but no gold or ivory or Japanese people dressed in silk and other finery to greet them. Nothing even resembled the descriptions of Marco Polo. Columbus's letter of introduction was useless here too. Was this, indeed, Japan or China?

Now the natives indicated that farther into the interior of their land gold could be found at a place called Cubana-can (*nacan* was dialect for city). Desperate to believe them, Columbus continued to mishear words, and now he felt certain that he heard the name Kublai Khan. So without delay he sent an embassy of men into the interior and instructed them to return within six days. Meanwhile, Columbus and the others made repairs on the caravels and spent time exploring and tasting local products—sweet potatoes (or possibly yams), kidney beans, and a grain the Indians called maize.

When the embassy returned, the men reported that the excursion had been a failure. All they found was a primitive village of fifty huts. Something else new and unusual was observed, however, but they were unaware of it then as a source of wealth. What they saw were "firebrands" smoked by the Indians. The Indians called them *tobacos*.

Disappointed and lacking the means to continue exploring the interior, Columbus prepared to depart. He was pained to leave this place and still have nothing valuable to bring back to Spain. He needed something to prove to the court that he had reached his destination. Just before departure he ordered the capture of several natives. He hoped that bringing back people from a variety of islands would help.

After the fleet put to sea, Columbus and his crew explored the northern coast. Columbus refused to believe Colba was an island. He now insisted it was the Asian mainland or at least a peninsula to China, and the other place called Bohío must be Japan. Difficult weather conditions prevented further coastal exploration, but Columbus figured perhaps it was just as well they make for Bohío.

Weather conditions worsened, and on a stormy sea the *Pinta* got lost from the fleet and completely vanished from sight. Columbus was angry. All along, Pinzón, the commander of the *Pinta,* had been headstrong and bold, "causing much trouble," and Columbus was sure he had wandered off to grab gold for himself.

By the first week of December the *Santa María* and the *Niña* reached the western most extension of Bohío, which shares Haiti (the western portion) and the Dominican Republic, to its east. The first port they stopped at was a fine, deep one with a clean bottom and good holding ground, but Columbus saw no promise here. At the second port they were attacked by mosquitoes and remained grounded there for several days because of wind and rain. But Columbus saw "grandeur and beauty" as well as fertile land. There, on December 9, he raised the royal banners and declared possession of the place he named La Española, little Spain; it came to be called Hispaniola.

During their stay Columbus took the opportunity to make contact with the Indians. He felt that he was becoming better at communicating with them, but as usual, the Indians were vague about gold.

By the third week of December the fleet was finally able

Columbus at Hispaniola, offering trinkets to the natives NEW YORK PUBLIC LIBRARY

to leave; however, strong headwinds pushed them into a channel, bringing them to a river mouth. Columbus called the spot Paradise Valley. There Columbus met one chieftain, whom the natives called the *cacique,* and then another chieftain who journeyed with tribal members in a dugout canoe from a nearby island, Tortuga. Columbus invited this

47

second chieftain on board to dine at his table in the stern castle. His guest ate and drank only part of what was offered him, arranging to have the rest of his servings delivered to his people. Columbus found him to be "marvelously content," and wrote in his diary that the chieftain "was much impressed and said to his councilors what great lords Your Highnesses must be, since they had sent me such a great distance without fear."

After the departure from Paradise Valley, they continued exploring the northern coast of Hispaniola, sailing eastward. On December 21, they anchored at a well-protected harbor that Columbus called Santo Tomás, in honor of the day, which was the feast of St. Thomas. Here the natives, the Tainos, were especially gentle and hospitable, offering their visitors all they could find, including fish, small earthen jars of water, and balls of spun cotton. The chieftain, Guacanagarí, took a great liking to Columbus and offered him a mask with ears, a tongue, and a nose of hammered gold. Later he sent three fat geese. Columbus made sure that he and his men pleased their hosts by being agreeable. He wrote that good relations were important for when the time came to convert the Tainos to Christianity.

Certainly good relations were established during those few days. When it was time for Columbus to depart, Guacanagarí and hundreds of Indians stood on the shore and begged the visitors to stay. But Columbus had heard of a gold-bearing region called Cibao, and he wanted to find it. Once again, Columbus heard what he wished to hear—the name Cipangu. "May God in His mercy help me to find this gold," the stubborn Columbus wrote.

How many tales would he believe? And for how long could he continue to search before meeting with disaster?

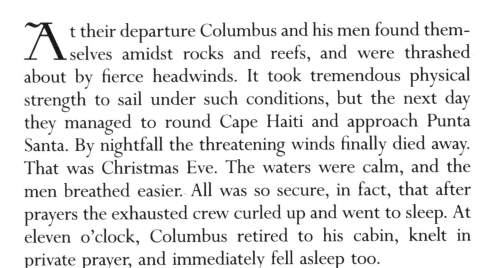

6

Shipwrecked

At their departure Columbus and his men found themselves amidst rocks and reefs, and were thrashed about by fierce headwinds. It took tremendous physical strength to sail under such conditions, but the next day they managed to round Cape Haiti and approach Punta Santa. By nightfall the threatening winds finally died away. That was Christmas Eve. The waters were calm, and the men breathed easier. All was so secure, in fact, that after prayers the exhausted crew curled up and went to sleep. At eleven o'clock, Columbus retired to his cabin, knelt in private prayer, and immediately fell asleep too.

The ship's master, Juan de la Cosa, was second in command. He was as weary as the others and decided to leave the ship in the hands of the helmsman. He instructed the helmsman to watch a bright star to keep on steady course and to waken him if wind or weather changed. Then he shut his eyes. Now the helmsman found himself nodding, so he shook the gromet awake to take charge. The tiller was heavy and hard to handle, but the helmsman thought it all right to entrust it to the young boy for a few moments. This, however, had been forbidden by Columbus.

A moon shone that night, but it was too low and dim to reveal white water breaking on dangerous coral reefs ahead. The gromet had his gaze fixed upon a star and didn't see the ground swell. It seemed as if the ship were hardly moving, but a gentle current was carrying it closer and closer to the reef. Then disaster struck. Suddenly the boy felt the rudder ground, heard the grinding sound, and cried out. Columbus and Juan de la Cosa leaped up, and one by one the sailors awakened and swarmed on deck.

Immediately Columbus ordered the men to drop anchor and pull on the capstan to back up the ship, a near impossible task. Columbus then ordered Juan de la Cosa to haul in the ship's launch, which carried the anchor and rope and which was towing astern, but again Juan de la Cosa failed in his responsibility. Instead of doing as he was told, he jumped into the launch with several seamen and made for the *Niña*. This enraged Columbus. He continued shouting commands to the crew to lower the mainmast and toss out the ballast and all nonessential cargo. But nothing helped. The undertow pushed the ship to shore and swung it into the rocks. Water came rushing through the punctured holes and the open planking, and began filling the vessel's hull.

It was too late to save the flagship. Without delay, Columbus directed the men into the launches, and they rowed to the *Niña*. There, crowded on the one remaining vessel, the sailors stood helplessly watching the *Santa María* sink. It was a tragic Christmas Eve.

At dawn they retrieved what they could of the cargo, provisions, and the ship's rigging. A message was dispatched to the loyal Taino chieftain, Guacanagarí, who is said to have shed tears upon hearing the disastrous news. At once he sent help by way of canoes and then arrived to offer his personal sympathy to the disheartened Columbus. Columbus invited him to share a dinner meal on shipboard, and when he noticed his guest admiring his own amber beads, a scarlet cloak, and a bottle of orange water, Columbus presented the items to him. Columbus thought Guacanagarí and the Tainos deeply affectionate people, and he had great respect for them.

After the meal, Guacanagarí brought up the matter of a nearby tribe deeply feared by his people. They were the Caribs, known to attack with bows and arrows and to feed on human flesh. The word *cannibal* later came from the name Carib. Columbus assured the chieftain that his people were strong and well-armed, and he called for a demonstration of archery and gunpowder to prove it. The gunpowder frightened the Indians on shore, but assured them of the white men's strength.

Then Columbus brought up the matter of gold. Guacanagarí understood how eager Columbus was to find it, so he presented Columbus with a gold mask and gestured to the nearby region of Cibao. Columbus was reassured by this. Always the optimist, he decided that the shipwreck "in truth was not a disaster, but great luck." It was the will of God. With the *Pinta* still gone, the one remaining vessel could not hold all the men, so some would have to stay behind. And this was the place, Columbus figured, where a gold mine would be discovered for them all.

Many offered and even begged to remain, but some thirty-nine were chosen. The master-at-arms, Diego de Arana, was left in command. Among those in his charge were a carpenter; a painter; a ship's caulker; a tailor; a surgeon; Rodrigo de Escobedo, the secretary; Luis de Torres, the translator; and Pedro Gutiérrez, the shipmate who claimed he saw the light Columbus sighted before the landfall. With the help of the kind Taino Indians, all hands built a fort with timbers and planking from the destroyed ship and stored it with provisions, including trading goods, artillery, and seedlings for planting crops. This became the first Christian settlement on these shores. Because it was founded on Christmas Day, Columbus called it La Navidad.

As soon as the fort was completed, Columbus prepared to steer course for Spain. With only one vessel now, he couldn't take the chance of exploring further. Besides, he needed to return to court before Martín Pinzón, who would no doubt take credit himself and avoid punishment for abandoning the fleet. It so happened there was word that local Indians had seen another "house on water," but after a search nothing turned up. Nevertheless, Columbus was worried, and following a farewell banquet with Guacanagarí, he left La Navidad the first week of the new year in 1493.

Columbus now had to figure out the best ocean route home. He had discovered and charted the trade winds that brought them west. Now, in order to go east to return home, he knew he had to avoid the trades or he would meet them head on. But he was uncertain as to where their boundaries lay. His plan was to cross them diagonally in a corridor, sailing north and then eastward. Columbus never worried that he wouldn't be able to return to southern European shores. This is one of the most remarkable features of his exploration: Heading for an unknown destination is one feat, but finding a way back home is quite another.

The return voyage began peacefully. Although Columbus had not been able to find a passage to the Asian mainland, still he enjoyed a sense of accomplishment, and he was sure that one more voyage was all he needed to meet with complete success.

Soon after the journey home began, someone on the

Niña sighted the *Pinta*. Martín Pinzón came aboard the *Niña* and immediately began to explain his long absence from the fleet. Columbus didn't believe any of the excuses, but he thought it wise to pretend that all was forgiven.

No sooner had calm been restored than they all found themselves once more in danger. Ahead was an island where they anchored to make repairs. But there they were met by terrifying-looking natives with charcoal-blackened faces and parrot feathers atop their heads. Columbus believed they were the dreaded flesh-eating Caribs. Immediately the Caribs attacked with a shower of arrows. When the Spaniards fought back, they wounded one native in the buttocks and another in the breast. With that, the Indians fled. But the incident marked the first clash between the Indians and the Europeans.

Columbus decided to depart because, he noted, "nothing is gained by staying here . . . and too many arguments have been taking place." That was in mid January. By the second week of February the caravels were back among the gulfweed in the Sargasso Sea and being carried farther north by the currents. Then a strong winter gale gave them a burst of speed as they neared the Azores at a latitude of 35 degrees. Fierce storms were characteristic of the region, and that winter was one of the worst ever recorded. The men watched the sea swell and the sky grow stormy. Soon the caravels began to roll and pitch, and amidst flashes of lightning, wave after wave broke on the decks.

"From sunset to daybreak [we] labored much with the wind and very high sea and tempest," Columbus wrote. All hands struggled to fill empty water casks to help make the caravels more stable and to lessen the chance of capsizing. Flares were lit so the *Niña* and the *Pinta* could keep contact, but on the second night of the storm, the *Pinta* disappeared again. Columbus's son Ferdinand later recounted that "when day broke they found themselves completely lost from each other's sight, and each ship must certainly have thought the other had gone down."

The storm raged on with such fury that no one on the *Niña* expected to survive, and the men prayed for their souls. If there should be a miracle and they should be saved, however, it was the decision that upon their first landing they would make a pilgrimage to a shrine. Columbus cried out to himself, and wondered why God should punish him now. So far, God had fulfilled his deepest wishes. He had lived through so many perils and come this far. Did the Lord want him to perish before he could bring home the news of his triumph? And was it meant for Columbus's two young sons to be left orphans in a foreign country? Columbus wrestled with his fears and anxieties, unable, as he wrote on that stormy sea, to "allow my spirit to be soothed."

Perhaps someone, somewhere at least would learn his story, he hoped. So in his hour of doom he wrote of what he had found on a piece of parchment, enclosed it in a waxed cloth, sealed it in a wooden barrel, and cast it out to sea.

But the *Niña*'s prayers were answered. The next day the winds shifted, and the sky cleared. Columbus and his men didn't know precisely where they were, but miraculously land lay ahead. Columbus guessed it was the Azores, and he was right. He would have preferred not to stop there because it was Portuguese territory, but they badly needed food, water, and rest. And from exposure to the cold and rain and from a lack of nutrients, Columbus's legs were numb and painful. Besides, the men had made a promise to the Lord, who had now delivered them from the storm, and several of them went to pray at the village chapel. Columbus's concerns about stopping in Portuguese territory were not unfounded. By order of the Portuguese governor, the men at prayer were seized in the chapel and taken prisoner.

A fragment of one of Columbus's many letters
LIBRARY OF CONGRESS

They were not released until Columbus's papers were inspected and declared valid.

Although Europe was not far away, Columbus and his men were still not out of danger. Just as they neared shore, a cyclone struck, splitting the *Niña*'s sails. Finally, Columbus managed to steer a course that helped them escape destruction. Many ships had been lost in the region that brutal winter.

Of course, they hoped to arrive in Spain, but instead another storm forced them to make port in Portugal. They were back in the hands of rivals. Columbus sent a letter to King John asking permission to land and tend to badly needed repairs on the *Niña*. Instead of granting permission, King John summoned Columbus to court, where the king lost little time trying to claim Portuguese rights to the conquest. Some members of the court urged King John to order the murder of Columbus, but the king decided against it, and Columbus left the court unharmed.

Columbus was anxious to reach Spain, still fearing that Pinzón had arrived first. As soon as possible, he set sail for Palos. Columbus was right about Pinzón. He had already returned; however, the sovereigns refused to receive him unless he was accompanied by Columbus. Distraught, Martín Pinzón went home and crawled into bed, and within a few days he died.

The glory Columbus dreamed of awaited him. Upon his return to Spain in the middle of March 1493, word spread quickly, and he became the subject of much attention. Meanwhile, he dispatched a long letter to the sovereigns describing his successes but avoiding mention of troubles. As soon as he received a royal reply to "come at once and make haste," Columbus set out by mule for Barcelona, where the court was held. He took with him several men in service, six captive Indians, a few caged parrots, some items he had collected, and a small sample of gold. It was a long journey, delayed by admiring crowds along the roads, who cheered Columbus and touched and pinched the strange-looking copper-skinned people.

At court Columbus received a royal welcome. A glorious procession and grand festivities were held to celebrate his return, and he was the honored guest at a solemn reception. Ferdinand and Isabella rose from their thrones, and with fervent gratitude bestowed great honor upon the explorer. Then they granted him his titles and privileges. "We confirm to you and your children, descendants and successors . . . offices of Admiral of the Ocean Sea, Viceroy and

Columbus at the royal court of Spain LIBRARY OF CONGRESS

57

Governor of the islands, and mainland you have discovered. . . ."

Columbus would never forget how people had laughed at his enterprise. And he would never cease to praise His Divine Majesty for guiding him and for bringing all good things to pass. As he received his titles from the Catholic sovereigns, Columbus felt well rewarded indeed.

Yet his discoveries worsened the rivalry between Spain and Portugal. By tradition, decisions about territorial expansion fell to the hands of the Pope. But Portugal refused to accept the Papal Bull issued by Pope Alexander VI. At Columbus's suggestion, the two countries met at Tordesillas, and there the matter was settled. A global line, *la raya,* was drawn down the 46th meridian (about 1,500 miles west of the Cape Verde Islands), giving all discoveries east of the line to Portugal, and all discoveries west of it to Spain, no matter which country made the discovery.

Of course to Columbus and to most Europeans his discoveries meant the East Indies. But there were a few doubters. One was a humanist and writer named Peter Martyr, who was an acquaintance of Columbus. He didn't necessarily think a new continent had been found, but he wondered if Columbus had come upon large, previously unknown islands near the East Indies. Few, though, paid attention when he wrote that he thought Christopher Columbus might have discovered "a new world."

Admiral of
the Ocean Sea:
The Second Voyage

It was clear to Columbus and the sovereigns that the task God intended had just begun. At court they discussed colonizing Spain's newly possessed land, and Columbus freely offered his views. He suggested that Hispaniola be secured with a settlement of at least two thousand people to start. He also recommended that three or four other towns be built nearby, each with a separate government and church for worship and for converting the Indians. Of course Isabella and Ferdinand were extremely pleased at the prospect of the Indians being "very ripe to be converted to our Holy Catholic Faith."

Plans were made at once for a second voyage, and the sovereigns drew up formal instructions. They included a call for the conversion of the natives, but they stipulated that the natives were to be treated "well and honorably." Some of the captured Indians, already baptized, were to go

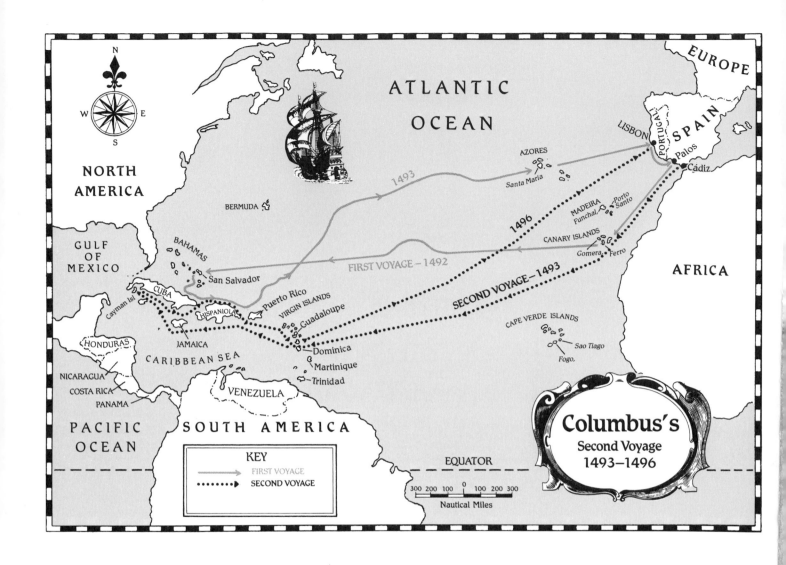

along as interpreters. The instructions also ordered further exploration of Cuba (which Columbus insisted was a peninsula to China) to find "greater good things, riches, and more secrets." They agreed to provide goods for a trading colony that would be established, with one eighth of the profits to go to Columbus while the rest would go to the Spanish crown. Private trade was prohibited.

Seemingly it never occurred to them, or to Columbus, that he would not be welcomed by the Grand Khan upon reaching China, or that it might be impossible to conquer the powerful leader and his people. Indeed, two centuries had passed since Marco Polo's journey, and there was no longer a khan, but an emperor of China instead.

In this naive way, the sovereigns and Columbus proceeded with their ambitious plans. This time the crown provided for seventeen vessels. With all the beating the *Niña* had taken, she remained such an excellent caravel that she was included in the second fleet, but renamed *Santa Clara*. The new flagship, like the shipwrecked one, was also the *Santa María,* but she was called *Mariagalante* and was larger than the other. The flagship's master was Antonio de Torres, brother to the nurse of the royal prince, Don Juan. Two other known ships were *La Gallega* and *Colina*.

Imagining immediate riches, hundreds of men clamored to sign on. Between 1,200 and 1,500 went, and they did so with the understanding that they would stay and build the colonies. Columbus, now Admiral of the Ocean Sea, was made Captain General of the Fleet. The archdeacon of Seville, Don Juan Rodríguez de Fonseca, was named administrator of financing and recruiting. Although described as "skilled in worldly matters," he proved to be unfriendly toward Columbus and other explorers.

Among the crew were Columbus's brother Diego; Juan de la Cosa, who had been on the first voyage; a soldier by the name of Diego Tristán; Columbus's steward, Pedro de Terreros; Dr. Diego Alvarez Chanca, a physician; Savonese Michele da Cuneo, a friend of Columbus's who went along for adventure; Nicolo Syllacio, a chronicler; Pedro de las Casas, father of Columbus's acquaintance, Bartholomew de las Casas; and a man by the name of Juan Ponce de León, who years later conquered Puerto Rico and sailed to Florida. Two friars also joined the voyage for the purpose of converting the Indians. No one from the Pinzón family went along, but several from the important Niño family of Palos did. And of course there were seamen, miners, laborers, and many peasants to work the land. Some of the vessels carried sheep and horses, which the men planned to breed on the colonies.

On September 25, 1493, with "weather and wind favored" they left the port of Cádiz amidst great fanfare and

61

pageantry. Both of Columbus's young sons were present that day, waving as their father and his large fleet disappeared from sight and made way for the Canaries. Gomera was the island on which they landed, and they stayed a week and a half, loading on large stores of provisions. Columbus was anxious to get back to La Navidad.

It was not going to be easy to keep a fleet of seventeen vessels together. So Columbus gave each captain sealed instructions on the route to Hispaniola, warning that they should not be opened unless the ship became lost. Columbus simply did not want the others to know *his* route. The course he set was west by south. It did not head directly for La Navidad, but, he hoped, would allow him to discover more islands en route since he had heard of a group of them located in the Caribbean Sea.

Three weeks later at sundown on November 2, Columbus was convinced that land was near. He ordered the fleet to shorten sail so as not to overrun land in darkness. He was right, for the next day, Sunday, they sighted a high, mountainous island, which Columbus named Domenica. The sailors sang the "Salve Regina" and shouted for joy. Dr. Chanca wrote, "They had all longed most fervently for land." Because there was no suitable place to anchor there, they did not stay. Instead they sailed on to another island Columbus named Mariagalante, after his flagship.

The following day they went ashore on an island Columbus named Guadeloupe. To their surprise, this turned out to be the island of the dreaded flesh-eating Caribs. But the Europeans did not flee, because they learned at the outset that most of the tribe was away on a raiding trip to other islands to capture women and boys. A few remaining Caribs and several other tribespeople, who were enslaved, managed by hand gestures to explain this.

Since the Europeans were in no immediate danger, a small group rushed into the interior of the island intending to plunder riches, but they lost their way in the woods. The search parties sent out to find them also disappeared. While Columbus awaited their return, he and some of the crew went exploring. They found geese and parrots and a fruit they had never tasted—pineapple. They also came across a wild fruit that caused painful inflammation of the face. It is believed to be the manzanilla, and it was what the Caribs used to make poisonous arrows.

In a further search, the men came upon huts in which they found bones and parts of human flesh. "The Caribs say that human flesh is so good that there is nothing like it in the world," Dr. Chanca wrote. He and other chroniclers of the voyage made detailed notes on the Caribs, describing some of their habits and customs; for example, they did not worship a God or idol, they slept on the ground, and they anointed their bodies, hoping to ward off mosquitoes. The chroniclers did not describe their observations of this flesh-eating tribe with any emotion or fear. Rather, they viewed the tribe as an interesting curiosity.

Columbus was about to give up searching for his lost men when they returned. The group of greedy men had been shown the way out of the woods by an old woman. Again there was no gold, and again the Europeans took natives, this time twelve young women and two boys who had been captured from another island by the Caribs. Columbus ordered that all dugout canoes the men could find be destroyed to stop further raids.

After leaving Guadeloupe they sailed across the Caribbean Sea, smooth and polished as a "blue marble," and made their way along the south coast of Puerto Rico to reach the north shore of Hispaniola. On this route they passed an arc of many islands, including a group now known as the Virgin Islands. However, it was impossible to explore them all.

Excitement was high at the prospect of seeing La Navidad and its progress. But upon their approach, no happy greeting awaited the crew as they had expected. In fact, there was little sign of life. When they anchored and went ashore, they found two corpses on the river bank. One had a rope of grass tied around its neck, and the other lay with bound feet. Because they had been dead for perhaps months, the bodies were badly decomposed, so it was difficult to identify them. Was this an evil omen? Fear pierced Columbus and his men. Farther along they found two more bodies. These were bearded. It was obvious now that they were Europeans.

Columbus's worst suspicions proved to be true. The fort had been burned to the ground, and the site was strewn with refuse and rotting corpses. Every man had perished.

Guacanagarí, the chieftain of the Taino Indians who had befriended Columbus during his earlier journey, sent regrets along with a message that he had tried to defend the Christians and was wounded as a result. Columbus and several men went to the chieftain and found that he did not have any serious wounds, and so they were convinced that he was not telling the truth.

Columbus had sincerely believed that a trust had formed between the Christians and the natives, but he saw now that the peaceful joining of these two different cultures had not come to pass. Little by little he learned that quarrels had sprung up when the Christians lusted for gold and also began to take Indian women. The Indians saw fit to defend themselves and their territory, and in the end the first settlement came to nothing more than a bloody massacre.

8

Beginning of Bloodshed

The men grieved the dead, but the immediate task was to find a more suitable and promising site to establish a permanent settlement. At the beginning of January 1494, they anchored at a village a short distance east of La Navidad. It seemed to provide a good harbor for shelter and a fine place for fishing, and there Columbus decided to build. He called the city Isabela. But his decision was made hastily, and in the end it was a poor choice for a site. The land was marshy, there was little protection from strong north winds, and it was a mile from the river, which proved to be unnavigable.

Columbus wanted as quickly as possible to go inland to the province of Cibao, where Indians had gestured that there was much to be mined. He hoped to send enough gold back to the court to prove that it was worth maintaining so large a fleet. Wasting no time, Columbus organized an expedition under the leadership of Alonso de Hojeda, a hot-tempered man but an able soldier. Hojeda and his men trekked over mountains and through narrow paths and dense vegetation to a stony area that did indeed yield some gold deposits from rock and sand. Columbus finally decided that Cibao was not Cipangu, because it was too long to be an island. He concluded that it was part of a continent and sent men to erect a fort at the entrance to the mining area. The fort was named San Tomás.

From the start, the disgruntled men knew nothing but trouble. They toiled among swarms of mosquitoes in humid and rainy climate to which they were unaccustomed and which also rotted most of their food. One by one they fell ill. Dr. Chanca worked such long, hard hours he demanded extra pay. Everyone was so miserable that finally Columbus dispatched twelve vessels to Spain with an urgent request to return three or four caravels with food, clothing, and medicine, more miners, and mules for hard labor. Columbus also sent samples of gold, cinnamon, and pepper, and twenty-six Indians to be baptized. This was apparently enough to please the crown, who agreed to provide all that Columbus requested.

The Christians were not the only ones who suffered. The natives of the region were deeply unsettled by the intrusion, and it was only a matter of time before conflict erupted. The Europeans freely stole from the natives, who were defenseless. In revenge one day, a small group snatched the clothing of three Christians at San Tomás while they were swimming in the river, and their chieftain did not punish them. So Alonso de Hojeda took it upon himself to set an example, and he did so with brutal force. He captured the chieftain and his brother, put them both in chains, and cut off the ears of an Indian in the village square. For the Indians this was a terrible injustice and the beginning of real bloodshed.

Columbus seemed to turn his head from all that was happening. He had left his brother Diego in charge of

Isabela and went off on his quest. Of the five vessels that remained, he took the three caravels—the *Niña,* the *San Juan,* and the *Cardera*—with sixty men to Cuba. They sailed through the Windward Passage, over emerald waters, breathing the delicate scents of the tropical air until they reached the southernmost point of the island. Columbus decided once more that Cuba must be the main continent, but again he was greatly disappointed. If he had gone farther north and explored the northern coast, he would have realized it was an island, and if he had sailed some ninety miles north from there, he would have reached the point of North America that is now Florida. If he had ventured west across the Yucatán Channel, he would have found himself amidst the splendor and wealth of Mexico.

But instead he sailed to nearby Jamaica. In all his journeys so far, he found it to be the "most beautiful island of all," but he found little else there. Under great strain, he went back to Cuba, encountering troublesome navigation, stormy weather, and a crew of hungry and restless men. He too was weary and wracked with doubts. But when his men expressed uncertainty that this was the East Indies, Columbus made them swear testimony under threat of physical punishment that Cuba was not an island, but a peninsula to the mainland. This was the act of a desperate man.

Columbus arrived back in Isabela in such a gravely ill state that he had to be carried ashore. He was pleased, though, to find his brother Bartholomew there. Bartholomew had been in France when he heard about the first voyage. He had managed to escape the pirates who had captured him, but he did not make it back to Spain in time to set out on the second journey. When he finally arrived, the sovereigns granted him use of three caravels that carried some provisions. But the caravels with the bulk of badly needed supplies that Columbus had earlier requested did not arrive until the end of the year.

While it was good to see Bartholomew, Columbus found all else at Isabela and San Tomás in "a pitiful state." The relationship between the Christians and the Indians had badly deteriorated. Columbus was afraid to take a firm hand and punish his men because of the public criticism such actions would bring about in Spain. He wanted to treat the natives well and honorably, but this grew increasingly difficult. The more he lost control of his authority, the more he tried to display power by ordering the natives punished.

Slave labor was already under way. The natives were forced to work the mines, and under the threat of cruel punishment they were required to produce a certain quota of gold dust. But there simply wasn't enough gold available to meet those quotas. The Indians were overworked and hungry, and in a short time they began to die. Some felt so hopeless that they saw no way out but suicide.

With such harsh treatment and growing unrest, it is little wonder that the Indians shunned efforts to convert them to Christianity. Also, the Indians could not easily understand a religion and culture that was so different from theirs. Moreover, Friar Buil showed little sympathy for the plight of the Indians. Neither he nor his fellow friar spent much time trying to baptize them, which was the reason the friars joined the voyage.

Under such troubling circumstances, Columbus began to lose control over his own men. They stole shamelessly from the Indians and committed atrocious acts. When one soldier, Mosén Pedro Margarit, was reprimanded by Diego, Margarit and several other mutineers seized Bartholomew's caravels and sailed for home. One of those mutineers was Friar Buil. Talk of mutiny was now everywhere. Columbus, still ailing, named Bartholomew in charge. This was deeply resented and became further cause for revolt.

Months and even years passed. By the beginning of 1496,

Some Indians preferred suicide to slavery. NEW YORK PUBLIC LIBRARY

Columbus and Bartholomew somehow managed to build three more forts in the interior. By then gold could only be obtained by laboriously washing it out of the sand and gravel in the river beds. Columbus felt he could reap no more from Isabela. (Today Isabela is a deserted forest, which some believe to be haunted. About 30,000 natives once lived on the island of Hispaniola, and by the time the Christians left, one-third had died or been killed.) He decided to catch the March westerly winds and return home. No doubt those who had returned earlier, including a man who had been sent to investigate complaints, were giving false reports about him in Spain, and this greatly troubled Columbus.

But his pain could not have been more profound than that of the natives. Before the return voyage the men seized hundreds of Indians, torturing and executing them, and then kidnaped thirty, including the chieftain. At the departure a hurricane (*huracán* is a Taino word meaning sudden storm) had destroyed all but the tough little *Niña,* and from the wrecked vessels, another was built—the *Santa Cruz,* nicknamed the *India.* The prisoners were naked, cold, packed in unbearable conditions, and almost starving. Their suffering knew no end. Food was scarce for all, and some of the Christians went so far as to suggest killing the Indians and eating them, but that was not done. Most died en route anyway, Columbus's friend Michele de Cuneo wrote, and were "cast into the sea." The few who survived in Spain were sold into slavery.

On June 11, 1496, the *Niña* and the *India* entered the Spanish port of Cádiz. There was no glory for Columbus this time. He was in poor health and felt so punished by God that he took to wearing a plain, humble Franciscan robe when he went to Burgos, where the court had recently moved. Despite concern over bad reports, the sovereigns greeted Columbus in a friendly manner. They also spoke of the possibility of yet another voyage, even though Columbus still did not know how he would find the passage to the Asian mainland.

9

Rebellion:
The Third Voyage

Columbus simply could not admit the possibility that he had discovered new land or reconsider his idea of the earth's size. He continued to believe that he had found a direct route to the East Indies. Certainly he had plenty of time to think about these matters before the next voyage, which didn't get under way for two years. But he remained stubborn.

Wars and weddings caused the long delay. France had invaded the Italian kingdom of Naples, and Spain was fighting to conquer the kingdom for itself. In addition, the Spanish sovereigns were involved in arranging marriages for their children. Prince Don Juan was marrying the Archduchess of Austria. Their younger daughter, Doña Juana, was marrying the Archduchess's brother. And their older daughter, Doña Isabella, was to become queen of Portugal through her marriage to Don Manuel, now the Portuguese king.

When the sovereigns finally authorized the voyage, their

instructions were not unlike those from the previous journey. The route, however, would be somewhat different. Columbus planned first to sail south toward the equator before going west. He had heard rumors of a land mass across the ocean from Africa, and he had also come to the conclusion that precious stones and spices lay in hot regions. Moreover, with this new route, he would avoid any rival French fleets that might be lying in wait to attack. This journey became known as the southern voyage.

With the stories that had come back from Hispaniola, recruiting was more difficult now. Columbus asked the king

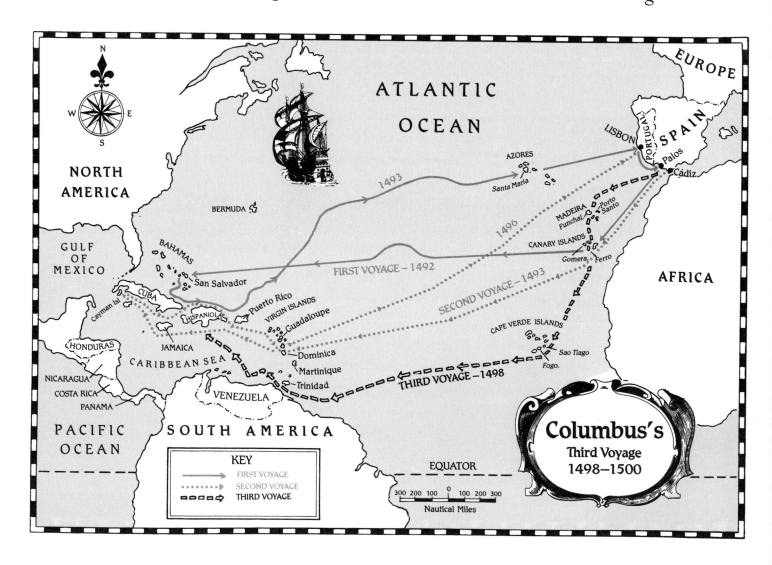

and queen to pardon criminals in exchange for their service on Hispaniola. Glad to save money on wages, they obliged by pardoning all willing criminals except those condemned for murder, treason, or arson. Columbus later noted that one pardoned man, whose ears had been cut off for a crime committed in Seville, remained well behaved throughout the journey. Another new crew member on the southern voyage was Bartholomew de las Casas, a twenty-six-year-old university graduate who later became the first priest ordained in the New World. It is said that a number of women also signed on without wages, but it's uncertain whether or not they actually went to sea.

Six vessels were outfitted. The flagship was the *Santa María de Guiá*. One caravel, *Correo,* was nicknamed *La Gorda,* and another, *La Castilla,* was nicknamed *Vaqueños.* The names of the other caravels are unknown. After the second voyage, the remarkable little *Niña* had met with an unplanned adventure. The story goes that both she and the *India* had been taken without permission by some Spaniards on a money-making mission to Italy. There they were captured by pirates. The *Niña* was stripped of her arms but was later recovered by the men who had stolen her in the first place.

After much debate, historians believe that the *Niña* made a third voyage across the ocean to Hispaniola with supplies. She was completely re-outfitted with new sails, planking, and equipment, and on the journey she was fully laden with wheat, wine, salt pork, sardines, cheese, olive oil, and nearly two tons of flour. It is further believed that she was sold in 1499, and there her recorded history ends.

Columbus's health was ever failing, and before his departure he made sure he had drawn up a will. All his titles and property were to be bequeathed to his older son, Diego; in case of Diego's death, the order of inheritance would fall to his younger son, Ferdinand and then to his brothers.

On May 30, 1498, the fleet departed from the port of

73

Sanlúcar de Barrameda. Three vessels sailed directly to the southern coast of Hispaniola, where Columbus's brother Bartholomew had earlier established a city named Santo Domingo. Under Columbus's command the other three vessels sailed south by way of the Cape Verde Islands. It was the admiral's intention to cross the equator and then follow a westerly course. "May our Lord guide me," he said in prayer, "and grant me that which may be for His service and that of the king and queen, our Lords, and to the honor of Christendom; for I believe that no man has yet taken this course and that this sea is altogether unknown."

They were about to cross the equator into the southern hemisphere, when at a latitude of five degrees above it, the endurance and faith of the sailors were again tested in a most terrifying way. Suddenly and unexpectedly, all winds ceased and left them in such "scorching heat" and "fiery furnaces" that they feared the ships would catch fire and all would perish. They lay still in these doldrums for eight days. The heat was so oppressive below deck that no one dared to go to check the casks of wine and water that had burst, or to toss overboard the salt meat that had become putrefied.

Finally, as Columbus wrote, the Lord saw fit to "grant excellent weather for escaping that fire." With the sudden rush of wind, the admiral set a course west on the latitude parallel to the African country of Sierra Leone, sailing seventeen days and bringing the vessels south of the Caribbean Islands. The sailors gave thanks to God for delivering them from the doldrums, but they grew alarmed at being so far from home in unexplored seas.

At the sight of an island with three peaks, which Columbus named Trinidad, for the holy Trinity, cheers went up. Because the island lay on the same parallel as the west coast of Central Africa, Columbus hoped to find people of very dark skin. Instead he found more Indians, although they were not entirely naked as were the Indians he had found on his first voyages, and some wore small gold ornaments. He realized there was no connection from there to Africa since the distance across the ocean was so great.

The region that Columbus was exploring was part of today's South America. Between Trinidad and the northern Venezuelan coast to its west lay the Gulf of Paria, into which both the Rio Grande and the Orinoco River empty. The men were grateful to find fresh water because it was badly needed. But the rivers further confused Columbus. If the land he had reached, Venezuela, were an island, how could it contain such large rivers? Also, if it were an island that could be linked to Cuba—which he still thought to be a peninsula to the Asian mainland—where was that link? At moments he even asked himself if Venezuela might be a continent, but he had trouble accepting that idea and dismissed it.

Columbus sent one of the caravels on a deeper search of the gulf, and she returned with the report that toward the westward passage there were four river channels. (The four channels were the mouths to the Rio Grande.) Columbus was exalted by this news. Where else could he have arrived but at the Earthly Paradise, as recorded in the Holy Scriptures? Columbus wrote that there in the Garden of Eden at the end of the great Asian continent "flows the source that gives rise to the four rivers, the Ganges, the Tigres, the Euphrates, and the Nile." He convinced himself of further proof by quoting the prophet Esdras from the Book of II Esdras in the Bible: "Thou didst command that the waters be gathered in the seventh part of the earth; six parts thou didst dry."

Columbus wrote to Isabella and Ferdinand, "I have come to believe that this is a mighty continent which was hitherto unknown . . . it is a wonderful thing and will be so regarded by all men of learning." Of course his mind was so fixed on Asia that he was unable to see anything else. But that mind,

75

fixed as it was, belonged to someone who possessed both genius and madness.

Relieved and encouraged, Columbus prepared to leave the Gulf of Paria, where, toward the end of his stay the voyager had found an abundance of pearl oyster beds. After gathering a small amount of pearls, Columbus decided to move on to Santo Domingo, the Hispaniola settlement built by his brother Bartholomew. Columbus's health had taken another bad turn, this time leaving him with painfully inflamed eyes and even periodic blindness, and he needed to rest.

Natives fish for pearl oysters.
NEW YORK PUBLIC LIBRARY

Roaring riptides and dangerous undercurrents made for extremely difficult sailing, but finally the three vessels passed out to sea. Their arrival at Santo Domingo was delayed further by more troublesome currents that first took them one hundred miles leeward from their destination. But once in Santo Domingo Columbus was rewarded at seeing his brother. He was also pleased to find that Santo Domingo was a well-chosen site; it had a sheltered harbor, fertile soil, and a navigable river with easy access to the ocean. Columbus had hoped that the settlement would be a peaceful spot to rest and regain his health and strength, but it was not to be. Here too he found only discontent, despair, and death. Moreover, active rebellion was under way.

The rebel leader was Francisco Roldán, earlier appointed by Columbus as chief justice. It was easy for Roldán to convince fellow Spaniards to join him since so many were fed up with the conditions and with the authority of Columbus and his brothers, whom they considered foreigners. Roldán even managed to recruit Indians to his side, although the first offensive attacks he planned to include them in ended in failure. Roldán and nearly one hundred followers escaped to an interior region called Xaraguá, where they schemed and plotted further and caused havoc among the native villagers.

Meanwhile, the three caravels that had earlier separated from Columbus arrived. Strong ocean currents also prevented them from landing directly at Santo Domingo and carried them farther west to the area near Xaraguá. Roldán saw the opportunity to recruit more rebels and to seize the caravels and return to Spain, but this latest attempt at mutiny was not successful.

Columbus grew more fearful about the continued threat of rebellion and decided to try reasoning. So he sent a message to Roldán, whom he cunningly called "dear friend," and invited him to a peace conference. Columbus offered Roldán and his rebels two caravels to return to Spain, but Roldán was equally cunning and made a number of demands before he accepted Columbus's offer. In the end, Columbus agreed to provide the two vessels for those who wished to leave while continuing to pay wages to those who stayed, which included Roldán. He also agreed to provide slaves to perform the hard work, and pardoned the rebels from charges of mutiny.

In turn, Columbus asked that the returning caravels deliver a sealed letter to Isabella and Ferdinand, in which he explained that he was sending back unruly and unreliable men, and requested the court to replace them with more religious souls. With this he hoped the sovereigns would not question his leadership abilities or doubt that all was going well. But Columbus was humiliated by having to give in to such wicked men. Furthermore, with only two caravels left that were suitable for exploration he could not return to the Gulf of Paria where his Earthly Paradise, his Garden of Eden, lay.

But the hot-tempered Alonso de Hojeda, who had cruelly treated the natives during Columbus's second voyage, did go to the Gulf of Paria. After returning to Spain, he set sail in 1499 with a secret copy of Columbus's chart, which he had managed to get, and a charter of royal permission to gather pearls from the region. Not only did he load up with jewels but on the way home he also loaded up with slaves whom he had captured on the Bahama Islands. Accompanying Hojeda on this journey was a man from Florence, Italy, Amerigo Vespucci. Vespucci took detailed notes, which would receive wide attention in the future.

While Hojeda was at sea and Columbus back at the settlement of Isabela, where he had sailed from Santo Domingo, the Spanish sovereigns were receiving new reports. Some said Columbus was a good admiral but a poor leader on land, and that he and his brothers were unfit to

Amerigo Vespucci UFFIZI
GALLERY, FLORENCE, ITALY

rule. Others called him a tyrant. Still others went so far as to report that Christopher Columbus, the foreigner, was behaving as if he were an enemy of the Spanish court.

Isabella and Ferdinand understood that there was chaos in the colonies, but they were alarmed by the idea that Columbus might be their enemy. They had no choice but to send a judge to investigate and deliver a full report. The judge they appointed was Francisco de Bobadilla, an obedient royal officer. They regarded him as a gentleman who would show fairness and granted him complete authority to act as he saw fit during his stay on the island.

Bobadilla arrived at Santo Domingo at the end of the summer of 1500, while Columbus and Bartholomew were still on the northern coast at Isabela. The first thing Bobadilla reported seeing was a gallows with two hanging corpses. He was told that they were rebels, and that there were five more mutineers awaiting execution. Bobadilla was horrified and ordered Diego Columbus, left in charge, to release the prisoners at once. Diego refused. This enraged Bobadilla. He ordered Diego to be put into chains, and seized possession of Columbus's hut and all his papers and belongings. To win over the men, he told them they were entitled to keep all the treasure they found, instead of turning it over to the Spanish government.

When Columbus and Bartholomew returned to Santo Domingo, they were shocked. The court-appointed judge showed Columbus his written orders, but Columbus would not be convinced. In outrage, he shouted that his credentials ranked higher. Bobadilla had had enough. Without further delay he ordered Columbus put into chains. Columbus was dumbstruck and did not move. No one else moved either, for not one man had the heart to take such action against their commander. Finally the cook stepped forward and fastened chains around the ankles and wrists of Christopher Columbus, the Admiral of the Ocean Sea. Had all of his dreams and hopes come to this?

Bartholomew was put in chains too, and now suddenly all three brothers were prisoners. Bobadilla assumed power and decided to return the three to Spain to stand trial. In early October they sailed for Spain, with Bartholomew on one caravel and Columbus and Diego on *La Gorda.* Columbus, stripped of all dignity, was left writhing in agony in his chains. *La Gorda*'s commander took pity and, once at sea, offered to release Columbus. But Columbus would not accept the offer. "I have been placed in chains by order of the sovereigns," he declared, "and I shall wear them until the sovereigns themselves should order them removed."

He continued to wear them at home in Spain, dragging them wherever he went. It was almost as if he wanted to show the world how an important and loyal man was being forced to suffer. The spectacle of him in chains was painful to watch and no less a terrible situation for young Diego and Ferdinand, who were pages at the court and who were being called "sons of the Admiral of Mosquitoes."

Although all seemed lost, Columbus was not of the nature or will to give up. If he could only explain his side of the story to the queen, he knew she would understand. So in secret he wrote her a letter, but addressed it to Juana de Torres, former court nurse to the sovereigns' children and sister of Antonio de Torres, master of the flagship from his second voyage. He knew that Juana was sympathetic toward him and trusted her to deliver his words to Isabella.

Columbus wrote a long letter. In it, he poured out his heart and soul to his "Most Virtuous Lady," telling her how he had served with love and devotion, listing all that he had achieved and lamenting the dishonorable and cruel treatment he was receiving. "Our Lord made me the messenger and showed me the way to the new Heaven and earth," he wrote. Then he went on to flatter the queen by saying that no one had believed in him except she, "who was enlightened and made to inherit it all as His beloved daughter." The world had given him "a thousand battles," he wrote further, and he had been attacked by Christians and Indians alike, yet he was always sustained by the miraculous consolation of the Lord.

Step by step, then, he explained the troubles caused by the evils of Hojeda, Roldán, and finally Bobadilla, who had inflicted the worst harm and humiliation against Columbus while he was doing his best to "uphold the rights of their highnesses." Columbus begged their highnesses to punish those men in order to regain his own honor. "Our Lord God still exists in His power of old," the letter ended, "and He will punish all in the end, especially the ingratitude of injuries."

When the king and queen heard about the chains, they

were upset and ordered Columbus to be freed and given money to purchase proper clothing so that "he could appear in court in a state befitting a person of his rank." Perhaps the sovereigns were more sympathetic to Columbus because all was not going well in their lives either. Their son, only nineteen years old, had died shortly after his wedding. Then their daughter, Isabella, who had recently become queen of Portugal upon her marriage, had died giving birth to her first child. And the infant had not lived long either. A pall had descended over the court, and the queen was overwhelmed with grief.

It was the end of 1500 when Columbus appeared at court in Granada. The humility and tears he displayed moved Isabella and Ferdinand to issue a royal mandate ordering the return of Columbus's papers and belongings. But they did not restore Columbus's titles of viceroy over discovered lands, which had been taken from him, and they refused to punish Bobadilla.

Columbus, of course, was deeply wounded. He couldn't understand how dismal his situation was. As if that weren't enough, he was made to suffer further when the sovereigns appointed someone else governor and supreme justice of the islands and mainlands of the Indies, the very lands he had discovered. They also gave other territorial jurisdiction to Vicente Yañez Pinzón and Columbus's enemy, Hojeda. The new governor, Knight Commander Nicolás de Ovando, sailed February 13, 1502, with thirty vessels and 2,500 men to join those already at Santo Domingo.

Bobadilla had stayed there with some 300 men who reportedly continued to live in shame. Bartholomew de las Casas bore witness to the actions of the "soulless" men on that and future voyages, and spent the latter part of his life writing about the mistreatment of the Indians in hopes of

Bartholomew de las Casas was horrified by the plight of the Indians. LIBRARY OF CONGRESS

seeing it end. "The Christians should have loved and admired them," he wrote, "but the Indians suffered and died in desperate silence . . . with not a soul in the world to turn to for help."

During the time of Columbus's third voyage, the fifteenth century had drawn to a close. Now the sixteenth century and the age of colonialism began. With the routes that Columbus had discovered, Spanish and Portuguese explorers were making new discoveries, conquering new territories, and putting forth new theories about the earth. Christopher Columbus was fifty years old. His hair had long since turned completely white. He was sinking lower and lower in health and spirits, but still he clung to his old beliefs. As long as there was breath in him he was determined to complete his mission and regain the honor he deserved. He begged the sovereigns for one more voyage— and contrary as it seems after all that had happened, they granted the request of the man adrift in his dreams.

10

The Most Dangerous Voyage

Columbus's fourth voyage, known as the high voyage, turned out to be the longest and most dangerous of all. It began in the spring of 1502 when the sovereigns, perhaps hoping to get rid of Columbus, bid him to "go forth speedily."

At his departure they gave him a letter of introduction to a man named Vasco da Gama, a Portuguese navigator who had just completed an historic journey of his own. Like Bartholomew Dias years earlier, Da Gama had circumnavigated Africa by rounding the Cape of Good Hope, but he went on to sail the Indian Ocean and reached India. With this, a sea route to the East Indies was finally established. Now Isabella and Ferdinand imagined that Columbus might meet up with Da Gama somewhere at sea, and they bid the two men to be friendly toward each other. Despite all the new knowledge gathered by explorers, it was still difficult for many to comprehend the vastness of the ocean and the unlikelihood of encountering other voyagers.

Four caravels in rather poor condition were outfitted. The flagship, whose real name is unknown, was called the *Capitana*. She was rigged like the original *Santa María,* but was considerably smaller. Columbus sailed aboard her, but his frail condition prevented him from acting as commander of the fleet. That position went to his loyal companion, Diego Tristán. On this voyage with Columbus was his son Ferdinand, who was barely fourteen at the time. Neither Columbus, his son, nor his brother Bartholomew drew a salary, so they were not listed on the official payroll.

Bartholomew sailed aboard the *Santiago de Palos,* nicknamed *Bermuda.* Her captain was Francisco de Porras, and he was accompanied by his brother Diego de Porras, who was named auditor and clerk. As a personal favor to the Porras brothers, a high member of the court whose influence could not be questioned by Columbus had recommended them to the fleet. This was unfortunate because they turned out to be not only incompetent but disloyal. In contrast, on board the *Bermuda* was Diego Méndez, a man who became a hero of the high voyage. The captain of the *Gallega,* Pedro de Terreros, had the distinction of being the only man to have sailed on all four of Columbus's voyages. He too proved himself to be a brave and loyal man. So did the captain of the *Vizcaína,* Bartholomew Fieschi.

In all, 140 men and boys put to sea from Cadíz on May 9, 1502. This was three months after the newly named governor, Knight Commander Ovando, had been dispatched to the Hispaniola town of Santo Domingo. To avoid trouble, the sovereigns had forbidden Columbus to visit there until he was homeward bound. But just as Columbus was approaching the coast of Hispaniola, other trouble was brewing.

With Columbus's extraordinary intuitive sense he was able to predict all kinds of natural events at sea. A friend, Michele de Cuneo, wrote that "at only seeing a cloud or a

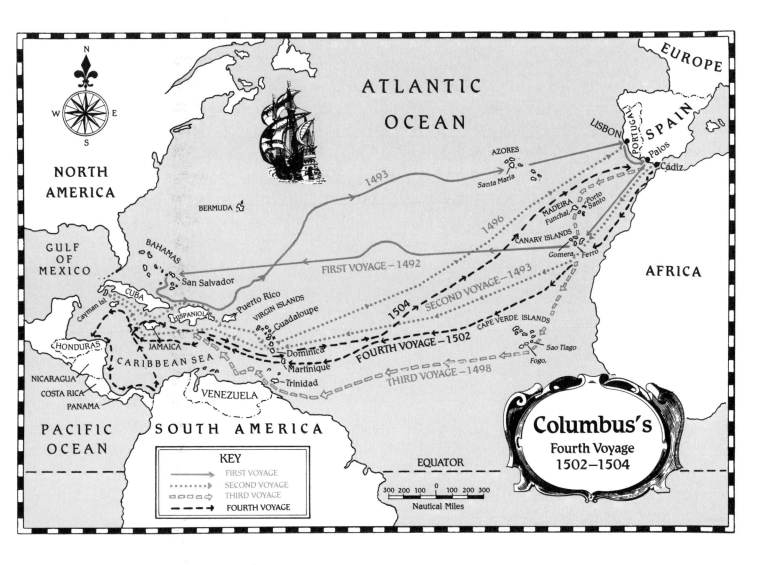

star at night, he indicated what was to come and if there would be bad weather." That is what happened on the last day in June. It was clear to Columbus that a hurricane was on the way. He knew all the signs. He could see long, oily waves rolling in, and he detected a heavy feeling in the air and an abnormal tide below. He observed veiled clouds, light gusty winds, and a crimson sunset, and he also noted how the seals and dolphins stayed near the surface.

The last thing Columbus wanted to do was ask Ovando for a favor, but he had no choice. So he sent a messenger ashore warning of the storm and asking permission to enter port and take shelter until it blew over. The messenger reached Ovando just before his fleet was preparing to depart for Spain. Ovando refused Columbus and ignored the warning. Ferdinand later wrote that his father became "full of bitterness in time of mortal danger to be denied refuge in a land he had given to Spain for its honor and exaltation." Columbus also lamented the suffering of his son, "so young a lad to undergo so much."

The best Columbus could do to protect his men was to anchor and take cover as close to land as possible. At the same time, Ovando's men weighed anchor and set sail. Then, as Columbus predicted, the hurricane struck. Violent, furious winds whipped and pounded them, tearing Ovando's fleet apart bit by bit and tossing one vessel after another into the churning sea. In all, twenty vessels went down, and not a soul survived. Only one caravel eventually reached Spain. Among the drowned were Columbus's enemies, Bobadilla and Roldán. Ferdinand called it Divine Providence, but Columbus's enemies at home declared that Columbus caused the hurricane by performing magic to take revenge.

Meanwhile Columbus's little fleet fought the hurricane courageously, and although they suffered damage, all on board survived.

After that the search for the mainland passage continued. At the end of July, they sailed west, crossing the Caribbean Sea, only to confront more storms and "constant punishment." Day after day, for four weeks they struggled heroically against the winds and currents that ripped the sails and rigging and destroyed most of the provisions. At last they arrived at Cape Honduras. By then the men wanted nothing more than to turn back. But Columbus would hear nothing of it.

Instead, throughout the fall months he took the fleet down the coast of what came to be known as Honduras, Nicaragua, Costa Rica, and Panama. The natives in these

Central American countries were clothed in fine garments, adorned with ornaments they crafted, and armed with swords. This was all quite new and intriguing, but what would truly have astonished Columbus and all of Europe was a nearby body of water that was unreachable by ship from the coast of Panama. Had they been able to cross the Isthmus of Panama, they would have discovered the Pacific Ocean.

By early winter, they ended up in a Panamanian coastal region Columbus called Veraguá. There just after the new year of 1503 began, they attempted to build a trading post near a river Columbus called Santa Maria de Belén (Bethlehem). Gold mines existed there, but it was impossible to extract gold from them because everything about the region was inhospitable. The few harbors were shallow and dangerous, the terrain was wild and rugged. Then the rainy season set in and brought terrible tempests and floods under a sky that Columbus said "blazed like a furnace." Moreover, the warlike Indians were becoming worrisome. They began appearing in bands and camping along the shores. Soon thousands assembled, and it became clear that they were preparing to attack the intruders.

Columbus's men were exhausted and defeated. The admiral himself was feverish and raving with malaria. It was decided to return to Spain for reinforcements. The loyal Diego Tristán, captain of the *Capitana,* was sent ashore to fetch a supply of drinking water for the voyage. He was rowing up the river when one of the bands of Indians sprang out from hiding and speared him through the eye, killing him. A fight began, and several others were killed as well. Now it was urgent to leave. But the *Gallega* was stuck on a sandbar and couldn't be moved quickly enough. In two days Diego Méndez built a raft to carry the men onto the other vessels, and the *Gallega* was abandoned. Méndez replaced Tristán as flagship captain.

The fleet could not reach Spain directly. They had to

stop first at Santo Domingo for provisions and repairs. Although Hispaniola actually lay north and east, the sailors believed it was due north, and so they made for it despite Columbus's better judgment and contrary equatorial currents.

It was April by then, and the wooden ships had been in tropical waters for a year. During that time, shipworms from those waters had invaded the submerged parts of the vessels and bored right through the planking, leaving them riddled "like honeycombs." The men used all receptacles available to pump out water, but this hardly helped, and they were left exhausted. The *Vizcaína* drew so much water she had to be abandoned. The remaining two vessels were not much better off. Hunger overtook the sailors too, partly because of other worms called weevils. The biscuits were so full of them that some men "waited until nightfall to eat the porridge made of them so as not to see the worms," as Ferdinand recalled.

The *Capitana* and the *Bermuda* were already on the verge of collapse when a violent storm hit. While laying anchor at a site between Cuba and Jamaica, the *Bermuda*'s mooring broke and smashed her stern into the *Capitana*. Following the storm, the vessels were completely crippled. All truly seemed lost. Yet, miraculously, they managed to stay afloat as winds helped them reach Jamaica. At the harbor, which Columbus named Santa Gloria, the men heaved the vessels aground, shoring them up on both sides so they could not budge. For shelter on the decks they built thatched cabins.

But what would come of them now? The food was gone. They were a hundred miles from Hispaniola, separated by a wide channel of rough waters. Santo Domingo was farther still. Although an Indian village lay nearby, there was no hope of anyone coming along to rescue them. There on the island of Jamaica they remained marooned.

90

11

"Inventor of a New Idea"

After deaths and desertions, 116 of the 140 men and boys were left. Columbus confined them to the grounded ships, trying to prevent troubles that would surely arise if they were allowed to roam freely. Fortunately the local Indians were the gentle Tainos who were eager to trade much needed food for trinkets. The relationship with them was civil at the start, but there was no telling how long this goodwill would last.

If anyone at Santa Gloria was to survive, it was necessary that a message reach Hispaniola. Even though it was a great risk, someone had to attempt canoeing across the channel. Diego Méndez offered to take that risk. With six Indians he set out in a dugout log, but they were attacked by other Indians and were forced to turn back.

Columbus begged him to try again, and this time Bartholomew Fieschi, the captain of the ill-fated *Vizcaína*, volunteered to accompany him. Now they used two dugout canoes and outfitted each with a mast and sail. The plan was that Méndez would proceed to Santo Domingo, and if all went well, Fieschi would return with news of their safe arrival.

When Méndez, Fieschi, and several Indians proceeded, not only did they face rough waters but they also had to cope with the height of the summer heat. Under the blazing tropical sun, terrible thirst and exhaustion from paddling overtook them. One Indian was left dead, and others lay seriously ill. At last, three days later, they made it to land. As planned, Fieschi intended to return to Columbus with news. But upon landing, several parched Indians drank so much water so fast that they too died. Few remained, and they had no desire to dare another perilous crossing.

Meanwhile, at Santa Gloria, the marooned lived day after day in misery. It was impossible to keep peace and calm. Illness, hunger, and fear of perishing could only result in revolt. The mutinous leaders were Diego and Francisco de Porras, who managed to sway forty-eight men to the rebel side. They attempted to escape in canoes, which had been stolen earlier to prevent the Indians from using them against the Christians. But the Porras brothers were poor seamen, and up against contrary winds they panicked. They had taken a number of Indians along, but in their panic they threw the Indians overboard. When the Indians clung to the canoes, the mutineers hacked off their hands. In short time they were forced to turn back. The mutineers were captured and the leaders put in irons.

By winter, any hope of rescue faded. The Christians, who ate much more than the Indians, apparently made no effort to grow their own crops, and the Indians grew tired of supplying them with food. The Indians were also showing signs of uprising. A most incredible story emerged at this time. It was the end of February, and Columbus remembered from reading an almanac that on the 29th of that year, 1504, an eclipse of the moon would take place. So Columbus sent for the chieftains and spoke to them. He said the Christian God in the sky was angry with them for neglecting to share their food, and He was planning to punish them. Some of the Indians laughed while others shuddered with fright.

Sure enough, on February 29 when the moon started to disappear, the Indians began to weep and beg forgiveness. Columbus told them he was going into his cabin to speak to the Christian God. There he remained until the eclipse was almost complete and he knew the moon was about to wax. At that moment he emerged and told the Indians that he had appealed to his God, who promised to return the moon providing the Indians "be good and treat the Christians well." As the moon reappeared, the grateful Indians offered thanks to Columbus and made good their promise to continue feeding the Christians. It was indeed a nasty trick, but one that Columbus found necessary for the Christians' survival.

Across the channel, Diego Méndez had managed to reach Santo Domingo where the new governor, Ovando, pretended he was glad to see him. He then stalled Méndez, faking an excuse that he was awaiting the arrival of more ships from Spain and could not spare one until that time. Finally, seven months later, he sent a caravel, but the vessel was too small to hold the lot of the stranded. More likely, he had sent it to spy on Columbus rather than as an earnest gesture of goodwill. Nobly, Columbus announced that all would be rescued or none, and so he stayed. The captain left a barrel of wine and a slab of pork, and sailed away.

Three more months passed before they were rescued, and the vessels dispatched to return them to Spain were not in good shape at that. By then Columbus and the survivors, whose number had dropped to one hundred, had been marooned one year and five days.

93

The homeward passage from Hispaniola began September 12, 1504, and ended November 7 at the port of Sanlúcar de Barrameda. Columbus, now fifty-three, returned to Spain a broken man. He suffered from arthritis, gout, and feverish delirium. But worse than the pain that wracked his body was his wounded pride. In a letter he had written at Santa Gloria and entrusted to Diego Méndez to deliver to the sovereigns, he poured out his anguish. He complained bitterly of the betrayal and "monstrous treatment" he had received during his earlier arrest. He begged his Highnesses to understand that after his long service to the sovereigns it was unthinkable that he would revolt against them, as he had been accused of doing. And he cried out pitifully, "May Heaven have mercy on me, may the earth cry for me, as I wait for death alone. . . . Hitherto I have wept for others; now . . . weep for me, whoever has charity, truth, and justice!"

But no tears were shed for Columbus. He was not even summoned to court. Isabella might have taken pity on him, but she was on her deathbed and died a few weeks after his return to port. It was said she died of a broken heart when her only remaining daughter, Juana, went mad. Columbus mourned Isabella. It is likely that he deluded himself that she would have restored his titles and privileges. It is likely, too, that he convinced himself that his honor and financial rewards would also be restored.

Ferdinand's court meanwhile moved from Segovia to Salamanca to Valladolid. Just as he had done so many years before, Columbus followed, waiting and hoping to be received. He managed the difficult travel only with the help of kindly friars and a few servants supplied to him by the court. When finally he was summoned, the meetings took place in haste. Columbus was paid a fair sum of gold for his efforts, but he felt he deserved more according to the original Santa Fé agreements. Ferdinand refused to restore

Columbus's titles, probably for fear that Columbus would then claim that he was entitled to further pay. Later Columbus and Diego petitioned the king to confer the ailing man's titles to his son, but Ferdinand continued to ignore the matter.

First page of the "Libretto," the first known printed book about Columbus. It is an account of his 1501 voyage. *BIBLIOTECA NAZIONALE MARCIANA AT VENICE*

Finally, at Valladolid Columbus settled into a modest, one-story brick house, with a small garden and fountain. There he was confined to bed, where he lay spent in raving fantasy. He was not penniless, for nearby he kept a box of gold. He also kept the chains that had once bound him and that he now morbidly requested to be buried with. At his bedside were his sons and brothers, his loyal friends Méndez and Fieschi, and a few devoted friars and servants. When he could no longer open his eyes, a priest was summoned. On May 20, 1506, as his son Ferdinand later recalled of his last hours, he "yielded up his soul to God on the Ascension," a holy day. The life of Christopher Columbus, the brilliant explorer who opened the unknown ocean to humankind, had come to a final, tragic end.

A small funeral procession passed quietly through the narrow streets of Valladolid, and a Mass was celebrated. Few realized the heroic proportions of the man who was being laid to rest. One who did, of course, was Bishop Bartholomew de las Casas. He thought Columbus "the most outstanding sailor in the world, versed like no other in the art of navigation, for which divine Providence chose him." But Las Casas was well aware that many in Spain at that time did not agree with him.

Columbus's story is a complicated one and impossible to think about without looking at its many sides. Columbus has been called a true genius, obsessed, faithful, weak, stubborn, patient, desirous of glory; he has been credited with opening up a new world and blamed for the enslavement of the new world by the old. Despite all the arguments, however, it is certain, as one historian, Paolo Taviani, says, that Christopher Columbus, Admiral of the Ocean Sea, did not become a discoverer by chance. He was a discoverer because he was also an inventor—"the inventor of a new idea."

12

After Columbus

No one knows for certain where Columbus was finally laid to rest. Many stories are told. According to his son Ferdinand, his body was transferred from Valladolid to Seville and buried in the cathedral of that city "with funereal pomp." About twenty-five years later, others have said, the body was transferred to Santo Domingo at the request of Columbus's heirs. Some believe this request was refused by Santo Domingo's bishops who would not bury Columbus there because he was "a foreigner." And some believe the request was granted, and that much later in the eighteenth century, when Santo Domingo was invaded by the French, the Spaniards whisked the remains to Cuba for safekeeping. The argument has long centered on the question of three final resting sites: Seville, Santo Domingo, or Cuba. Recently, however, a fourth possibility has been considered—perhaps Columbus's body never left Valladolid at all.

King Ferdinand eventually granted Columbus's titles to

Monument to Columbus at
Punta Del Sebo, Spain
PROVINCIAL FOUNDATION OF
TOURISM, HUELVA, SPAIN

his son Diego and temporarily appointed him governor of
Santo Domingo. In the end, however, the arrangement
came to no good. Ferdinand was the last royal witness to
Columbus and the enterprise. His successor to the throne,
Charles V, had never met Columbus or Diego, and he

ordered Diego back to Spain. After Diego's death, his son, Luis, sold his grandfather's memoirs and squandered the money. Columbus's son Ferdinand lived for a while on Hispaniola, but soon returned to Spain, where he studied and then held a number of government positions. He never married and left no heirs. His vast collection of books and manuscripts was left to a Seville cathedral, where, unfortunately, much was allowed to deteriorate.

New Views of the World

Certainly Columbus was the man who explored and conquered the Atlantic Ocean. But centuries earlier other daring navigators had sailed the Atlantic by celestial navigation to Iceland, Greenland, Newfoundland, and North America. These navigators were Norsemen, Scandinavian seafaring people. The Vikings were also Norsemen who were sea raiders. For three centuries, they raided and attacked the peoples who lived in the Baltic and North Sea regions.

Erik the Red was not a sea raider, but he was expelled from Iceland for killing a man, and he sailed to Greenland and established a settlement there. That took place in the tenth century. His son, Leif Eriksson, later established a settlement in Newfoundland. Historians believe that Norsemen also established a settlement in North America on the coast of New England, and archeologists are still searching for artifacts, hoping to find proof of the exact site. However, the Norsemen, whose ventures are known mostly by stories passed down through the centuries, are not considered discoverers of the Atlantic Ocean, because no views of the world were changed as a result of their journey to North American shores.

Columbus's historic voyage brought about a number of significant changes. First, it altered prevailing views of the world by demonstrating that the world was much larger and contained a great deal more water than was previously thought. Second, explorers could now investigate in all directions of the world and know that they could return home. As a result, mapmaking and the study of geography flourished.

Columbus's discovery of a new continent led to other far-reaching changes as well. The great quantities of gold and silver later found in the new land created the beginnings of world trade. These precious metals became the main source of trade, and in Europe they replaced land ownership as the most important means of wealth and power. Also, European settlers became aware of new forms of political life when they encountered the Indians' democratic methods of governing themselves; before then, Europe had known only the harsh rule of monarchies and aristocracies.

Furthermore, the Europeans were influenced by the Indians' agricultural and medical skills. The Indians cultivated a variety of vegetables, fruits, nuts, and oils, which enhanced the world's diet, and developed helpful techniques of processing their food. They also produced quantities of medicines from plants to fight diseases unknown to them before the arrival of the Europeans. One such medicine was quinine, which is effective against malaria. Columbus's discovery of a land rich in natural resources and populated by Indians with their own unique culture made a permanent and profound impact on the world.

How America Was Named

In 1499, while Columbus was on his third voyage, Italian astronomer and cosmographer Amerigo Vespucci sailed with one of Columbus's enemies, Alonso de Hojeda. Vespucci wrote an important narrative of that journey, but dated it 1497, two years earlier. Moreover, he made no mention of Columbus. He wrote: "Our ancient forebears thought that there were no continents to the south beyond the equator, only the sea they called the Atlantic. . . . My voyage has made it plain that this opinion is erroneous and contrary to the truth. For in those regions I have found a continent more densely populated. . . . We may rightly call this continent the New World." He meant Paria on the coast of South America, where Columbus had landed years before. Was Vespucci trying to attribute the discoveries to himself? That question remains difficult to answer.

This is what happened afterward. Vespucci's narrative was published in Latin and Italian, and a group of men in the French city of Saint-Dié became interested in it. One was a clergyman, Martin Waldseemüller. In 1507, Waldseemüller published a work called *New Introduction to Cosmography,* which included Vespucci's commentary. It also included the first map to show the new land, now called the West Indies. Waldseemüller suggested that the land discovered by Amerigo Vespucci be named after him. The invention of the printing press in the 1450s had hastened distribution of books throughout Europe, and this one became quite popular. In a short time Waldseemüller learned that it was Columbus who had made the discovery, but it was too late. The book had sold so many copies that he could not recall them to make the change. People everywhere were already calling the land America. The name of Columbus began to fade, and none of his heirs was able to protect it.

The First European To Find the Pacific Ocean

Vasco Núñez de Balboa was a Spanish explorer who sailed to Hispaniola and South America after Columbus's first three voyages. He never met up with Columbus, however. A few years after Columbus's death, Balboa hid aboard a ship leaving Hispaniola to escape from trouble with the law. When the stowaway was discovered aboard, he was first threatened and then pardoned by the captain whom he later overtook by force. Balboa was determined to find gold. He led a crossing through the Isthmus of Panama, which Columbus had been unable to reach by ship. Balboa's crossing took the expedition over rugged mountains and through tropical rainforests and infested swamps. Several of his men died from disease or clashes with natives. On September 25, 1513, on the other side of the Isthmus, Balboa climbed atop a mountain and gazed out over the Pacific Ocean. He then took possession "of all that sea and the countries bordering on it." He also found gold and pearls, which brought him the king's favor. Several years later a rival accused him of treason against the Spanish crown, and Balboa was beheaded in a public square.

The First Voyage Around the World

Columbus insisted his sought-after passage to the East Indies was in the northern hemisphere. But a Portuguese naval officer, Ferdinand Magellan, sailing under the Spanish flag, found the strait by way of the southern route. That was some thirty years after Columbus's first voyage. By then navigational instruments had improved. Also, understanding of the world was slowly progressing, although the width of the ocean Balboa had sighted was still a mystery.

The extraordinary and terrifying voyage of Magellan began with 234 men in five old, leaky vessels. When they neared the southern tip of South America, Magellan succeeded in finding a strait that turned out to be 334 miles of narrow, twisting passages, hazardous gorges, and extreme rough seas. The crews were more mutinous than Columbus's rebels, and the hunger and thirst of the thirty-eight-day ordeal was withstood only by the heartiest. At the end of the strait when they entered the Pacific, which Magellan named for the peaceful waters, the treacherous journey was far from over. Magellan estimated the width of the ocean to be 600 miles from the west coast of South America to the Spice Islands (the Molucca Islands) on the Malay Peninsula, which he figured were "no great distance from Panama." The distance, however, turned out to be more than 11,000 miles. The disease known as scurvy, caused by a lack of Vitamin C in the diet, and starvation claimed the lives of most of the sailors.

Unfortunately, Magellan was unable to complete his voyage. He had made it around the globe as far as the Philippine Islands, but there he became embroiled in a local fight and was speared to death. By that time there were only forty-seven crew members left. One, Juan Sebastian el Cano, continued on aboard the *Victoria,* and with only eighteen survivors managed to make it back to European shores.

The year of this historical journey was 1522. The passage through which Magellan sailed from the Atlantic to the Pacific was named the Strait of Magellan. This explorer of iron courage was the first to sail successfully all the way around the world. Now there was final and undisputable proof not only that the world was round, but that the globe was circumnavigable, as Columbus had believed.

The Death of the Indians

Bishop Bartholomew de las Casas spent forty years in the colonies. At the start he believed that slavery was justified. But in due time after witnessing prolonged cruel treatment of the Indians he began to speak out against it. He wrote at length in *The Devastation of the Indies,* not only of the horror of slavery but of the unjustified brutal killing of native men,

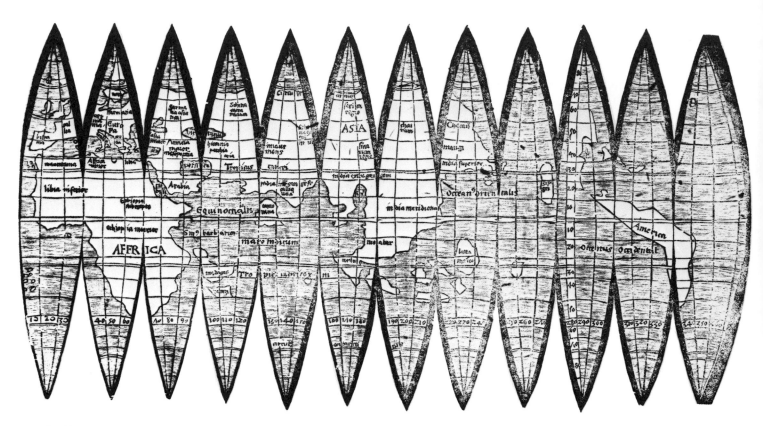

Waldseemüller's map—the first time the word "America" appeared on a map JAMES FORD BELL LIBRARY, UNIVERSITY OF MINNESOTA

women, and children. Las Casas devoted the rest of his life to protecting the Indians by calling for the passage of laws in Spain and overseeing their enforcement. But he did not succeed. Within a half century after the Christians set foot on the West Indies and the Americas, millions of Indians had been starved to death, ravaged by disease, or slaughtered.

Celebrating Christopher Columbus

It took nearly a century after Columbus's voyages before the world fully grasped both the existence of a new continent and a universe that was much larger than once believed. And it took nearly a century beyond that before the name of Christopher Columbus emerged again. That came about in the eighteenth century, largely as a result of

AFTER COLUMBUS

discussions among men in academic institutions. The aca-
demicians began to focus on Columbus and the Spanish
colonization of the New World. Documents were collected,
and biographies and other treatises were written. The
Catholic Church also played an important role in bringing
attention to Columbus, whom it praised as a man devoted
to spreading the Christian gospel. Certainly the academi-
cians and the Church did not dismiss Columbus's personal
faults or the problems that plagued him and damaged his
fame. But they established beyond any doubt that Columbus was indeed the master mariner and bold adventurer
who conquered the Atlantic Ocean and discovered America. Today the name of Christopher Columbus and his idea
are celebrated worldwide.

Chronology of Events

1451 (exact date unknown)	Birth of Christopher Columbus in Genoa, Italy
ca. 1466	First experiences at sea
1474–1475	Joins sea expeditions from Genoa to the island of Chios (Khios)
1476–1485	Lives in Lisbon, Portugal
1476–1477	Voyages from Lisbon to England and Iceland; first experiences high seas
1479	Marriage of Columbus to Doña Felipa Perestrello y Moniz, in Lisbon
1480	Birth of first son, Diego, to Columbus and Felipa, at Porto Santo
1483–1492	Devotes time and energy toward plan to seek short sea route to the East Indies by sailing west; plan is called Enterprise of the Indies
1484	Death of Columbus's wife, Felipa
1485	Leaves Portugal with son to live in Spain
1486	Received by Queen Isabella of Spain for the first time; presents plan for voyage

1486	Talavera Commission appointed to study plan
1488	Birth of second son, Ferdinand, to Columbus and Beatrice Enriquez de Arana
1492, April 17	Contract for voyage signed between Columbus and the king and queen of Spain, Ferdinand and Isabella
August 3	Sets sail on first Atlantic Ocean voyage, from Spanish port at Palos
October 12	Columbus discovers America; historic landfall on an island in the Bahamas
1493, March 15	Returns to Palos from first voyage
September 25	Sets sail on second voyage from port at Cádiz
1496, June 11	Returns to Cádiz from second voyage
1498, May 30	Sets sail on third voyage from Sanlúcar de Barrameda
1500, November 3	Returns to Cádiz from third voyage
1502, May 9	Sets sail on fourth voyage from Cádiz
1504, November 7	Returns to Sanlúcar de Barrameda from fourth voyage
1506, May 20	Death of Christopher Columbus, at Valladolid, Spain

Articles of Capitulation

Written by Queen Isabella and King Ferdinand, April 30, 1492, before the first voyage:

Don Ferdinand and Doña Isabella, by Grace of God King and Queen of Castile, Leon, Aragon, Sicily, Granada, Toledo, Valencia, Galicia, Majorca, Seville, Sardinia, Cordova, Corsica, Murcia, Jaén, Algarve, Algeciras, Gibraltar, and the Canary Islands;

Whereas you, Christopher Columbus, are setting forth by Our Command to discover and acquire with certain Vessels and people of Ours certain Islands and Mainland in the Ocean Sea; and it is hoped that with the help of God some of the Islands and Mainland in the Ocean Sea will be discovered and acquired by your efforts and industry, and so it is just and reasonable that, since you are endangering yourself in Our Service, that you be rewarded. Desiring to honor and favor you, it is Our will and pleasure that after you, Christopher Columbus, have discovered and acquired the Islands and Mainland in the Ocean Sea, you shall be Our Admiral of the Islands and Mainland and shall be Our Admiral and Viceroy and Governor, and shall be empowered to call and entitle yourself Don Christopher Columbus. And your Sons and Successors in the office and charge shall be empowered to entitle and call themselves Don, and Admiral, and Viceroy and Governor. And, that you shall have the right to exercise and enjoy the office of Admiralty together with the office of Viceroy and Governor of the Islands and Mainland that you may so discover and acquire, and to hear and decide all suits and cases, civil and criminal pertaining to the office of Admiralty and Viceroy and Governor according as you shall find by law and as the Admirals of Our Kingdoms are accustomed to use and exercise it; and shall have power to punish delinquents . . . and that you shall have and levy the fees and salaries pertaining to said offices and each according as Our High Admiral in the Admiralty of Our Kingdoms is accustomed to levy them.

And, by this our patent or a copy thereof, signed by a public notary, we command Prince Don Juan, Our very dear and beloved son, and all Princes, Dukes, Prelates, Marquesses, Counts, Masters of Orders, Priors, Commanders, and also members of Our Council, Mayors and other Magistrates . . . executive officials of all the cities and districts in Our Kingdoms and Dominions and of those which you may conquer and acquire; and also captains, masters, quarter-masters, mates and marine officials and seamen, Our natural subjects present or future, that after your discovery and acquisition of the Islands and Mainland, and after the administering of the oath and the performing of the rites prescribed by you or your deputy, they shall have and hold you henceforth, during the whole of your life and thereafter your son and successor after successor forever, as Our Admiral of the Ocean Sea and as Viceroy and Governor of the Islands and Mainland which you, Don Christopher Columbus, shall discover and acquire and they shall use toward you and your deputies in office of Admiralty and Viceroy and Governor, all honors, graces, favors . . . and also pay you and cause to be paid all dues pertaining to and deriving from the offices. . . .

Given in Our City of Granada, on the 30th day of April A.D. 1492.

I THE KING   I THE QUEEN

I, Juan de Coloma, Secretary to the King and Queen, our Lords, had this written by their command.

Letter of Introduction

Written on April 30, 1492, by Queen Isabella and King Ferdinand and carried in several copies by Columbus on his voyages to present to rulers of kingdoms he expected to meet:

To the Most Serene Prince [a blank space was left for Columbus to insert the names, since neither he nor the Spanish Sovereigns knew whom Columbus might encounter*] Ferdinand and Isabella, King and Queen of Castile, Aragon, Leon, Sicily, and so on, greetings and continued good fortune. From the statements of certain of Our subjects who have come to Us from Your Kingdoms and Domains, We have learned with joy of Your esteem and high regard for Us and Our nation and of Your eagerness to be informed of matters with Us. We have resolved to send you Our Noble Captain, Christopher Columbus, bearer of these, from whom You may learn of Our good health and Our prosperity he is ordered to tell you. We pray You to give good faith to his reports as You would to Ourselves, which will be most grateful to Us. We declare ourselves prepared to please you. From Our City of Granada, 30 April A.D. 1492.

I THE KING   I THE QUEEN

Coloma, Secretary

* The Spanish Court, as did many Europeans, still believed that the ruler of China was called the Grand Khan, as he had been two hundred years earlier when Marco Polo visited. But they were unsure of the proper form of address, so a blank space was left. In fact, the correct title at the time Columbus sailed was Emperor of China.

Crew on the First Voyage

Santa María

Christopher Columbus (Cristóbal Colón), admiral
Juan de la Cosa, ship owner and master of the ship
Peralonso (Pedro) Niño, pilot
Diego de Arana, master-at-arms
Rodrigo de Escobedo, admiral's secretary
Pedro Gutiérrez, steward
Rodrigo Sánchez de Segovia, paymaster
Luis de Torres, interpreter
Juan Sánchez, physician
Chachú, boatswain (master's deputy)
Bartolomé García, boatswain
Domigo de Lequeitio, boatswain's mate
Antonio de Cuellar, carpenter
Domingo Vizcaino, able seaman and cooper
Lope (Lupe), caulker
Juan de Medina, able seaman and tailor
Diego Pérez, able seaman and painter
Bartolomé Biues (or Vives), able seaman
Alonso Clavijo (criminal granted amnesty)
Gonzalo Franco, able seaman
Juan Martínez de Acoque, able seaman
Juan de la Placa (Plaza), able seaman
Juan Ruíz de la Peña, able seaman
Bartolomé de Torres (criminal granted amnesty)
Juan de Jérez, able seaman
Rodrigo de Jérez, able seaman
Pedro Yzquierdo de Lepe (criminal granted amnesty)
Juan de Moguer (criminal granted amnesty)

Cristóbal Caro, silversmith
Diego Bermúdez, apprentice seaman
Alonso Chocero, apprentice seaman
Rodrigo Gallego, servant
Diego Leál, apprentice seaman
Pedro de Lepe, apprentice seaman
Jacomél Rico, apprentice seaman (from Genoa)
Martin de Urtubía, apprentice seaman
Andrés de Yebénes (?), apprentice seaman
Juan, apprentice seaman, servant
Pedro de Terreros, steward's mate
Diego de Salcedo, ship's boy

Niña

Vicente Yañez Pinzón, captain
Juan Niño, master and ship owner
Sancho Ruiz (de Gama?), pilot
Maestre Alonso, surgeon
Diego Lorenzo, steward
Bartolomé García, boatswain
Alonso de Morales, carpenter
Juan Romero, able seaman
Rui García, able seaman
Rodrigo Monge, able seaman
Juan Arias, from Portugal
Bartolomé Rodan, able seaman
Juan Romero, able seaman
Pedro Sanchez de Montilla, able seaman
Pedro de Villa, able seaman
García Alonso, apprentice seaman
Andrés de Huelva, apprentice seaman
Francisco Niño, apprentice seaman
Pedro de Soria, apprentice seaman

Fernando de Triana, apprentice seaman
Miguel de Soria, apprentice seaman and captain's servant
Alonso Gutiérrez
Gutiérrez Pérez
Juan Ortíz

Pinta

Martín Alonso Pinzón, captain
Cristóbal Quintero, owner with able seaman's rating
Francisco Martin Pinzón, master
Cristóbal García Sarmiento, pilot
Juan Reynal, marshal or master-at-arms
Maestre Diego, surgeon
García Fernández, steward
Juan Quintero de Algruta, boatswain
Antón Calabrés, able seaman (from Calubria)
Francisco García Vallejo, able seaman
Alvaro Pérez, able seaman
Gil (or Gutiérrez?) Pérez, able seaman
Diego Martín Pinzón, able seaman
Juan Bermúdez, from Palos
Sancho de Rama, able seaman
Gómez Ráscon, able seaman
Juan Rodríguez Bermejo (also known as Rodrigo de Triana)
Juan Vecano, able seaman (from Venice)
Juan Verde de Triana, able seaman
Pedro de Arcos, apprentice seaman
Fernando Méndes, apprentice seaman (from Huelva)
Francisco Méndes, apprentice seaman (from Huelva)
Alonso de Palos, apprentice seaman
Juan Quadrado, apprentice seaman
Pedro Tejero, apprentice seaman
Bernal, apprentice seaman and captain's servant

Suggested Reading

Boorstin, Daniel J. *The Discoverers: A History of Man's Search to Know His World and Himself.* New York: Random House, 1983.

Columbus, Christopher. *The Log of Christopher Columbus.* Translated by Robert H. Fuson. Camden, Maine: International Marine Publishing Co., 1987.

Judge, Joseph et al. "Where Columbus Found the New World." Special edition of *National Geographic Magazine,* vol. 170 (November 1986).

Keen, Benjamin, trans. and annotated. *The Life of the Admiral Christopher Columbus by His Son Ferdinand.* New Brunswick, N.J.: Rutgers University Press, 1950.

Martinez-Hildalgo, Jose. *Columbus's Ships.* Barre, Mass.: Barre Publishers, 1966.

Morison, Samuel Eliot. *Admiral of the Ocean Sea.* Boston: Little, Brown, 1942.

————. *The Great Explorers, the European Discovery of Americas.* New York: Oxford University Press, 1978.

————, ed. *Journals and Other Documents in the Life Voyages of Christopher Columbus.* New York: Heritage Press, 1963.

Polo, Marco. *The Travels of Marco Polo.* Translated by Ronald Latham. New York: Penguin Books, 1958.

Preston, Edna Mitchell. *Marco Polo.* New York: Crowell Collier, 1968.

Robinson, M. Gregg. *Rival Cities, Venice and Genoa.* New York: McGraw-Hill, 1969.

Taviani, Paolo Emilio. *Christopher Columbus, The Grand Design.* London: Orbis Publishers, Ltd., 1985.

Weatherford, Jack. *Indian Givers, How the Indians of the Americas Transformed the World.* New York: Crown, 1988.

Index

Page numbers in italics refer to illustrations.

Africa, 7, 74–75
 circumnavigation of,
  3
 Portuguese trade
  with, 5–6
Alexander VI, Pope,
 17, 18, 58
Alfonso V, King of
 Portugal, 3, 5
America, naming of,
 100–101, *104*
Asia, *see* East Indies
Azores, 5, 7–8, 53, 54,
 56

Bahama Islands, 40–
 44, 78
Balboa, Vasco Núñez
 de, 101–102
Barcelona, 56–58
*Bermuda (Santiago de
 Palos)*, 86, 90
Bobadilla, Francisco
 de, 79–82, 88

Cádiz, 61–62, 86
Canary Islands, 4, 7,
 28–30, 63
Cape Verde Islands, 5,
 58, 74
Capitana, 86, 90

caravels, 7, 15, 23, 28,
 67, 68
 for fourth voyage,
  86
 for third voyage,
  73, 75, 77, 78
Caribbean Sea, 62, 63,
 88
Caribs, 51, 53, 62–63
Catholicism, 17–18,
 27, 33, 35, 54
Chanca, Diego
 Alvarez, 61, 62,
 63, 66
Charles V, King of
 Spain, 98–99
China, 12, 30, 60
Christianity, spreading
 of, 17–18, 21,
 42, 48, 59, 61,
 68
Christopher, Saint, 11,
 11
Cibao, 48, 51, 65–66
Cipangu (Japan), 30,
 36, 43, 45, 48,
 66
Columbus,
 Bartholomew, 2,
 6, 8, 19, 86

in Hispaniola, 67–
 68, 69, 74, 76,
 77, 80
Columbus,
 Bianchinetta, 2
Columbus,
 Christopher:
 accomplishments
  of, 99–100
 aging of, 84, 94
 appearance of, 4, *4,*
  84
 birth of, 1
 Bobadilla's
  investigation of,
  79–80
 books as influence
  on, 9, 12–14
 as cartographer, 6
 in chains, 80–82,
  96
 critics of, 78–79,
  88
 death of, 96, 97
 debts of, 15
 early seafaring
  experiences of, 2,
  4–5, 7
 education of, 2, 6, 8
 fame and glory of,
  56–58, 104–105

health problems of,
 54, 67, 70, 73,
 76, 77, 84, 94
intuition of, 4, 65,
 86–87
letters of, 10, 54,
 55, 56, 75, 78,
 81, 94
loss of authority by,
 66, 68
marriage of, 7
mental and spiritual
 adventure of, 7–
 11
monument to, *98*
New World landing
 by, *40*
optimism of, 31, 51
in Portugal, 5–7,
 15, 36, 56
powers of
 observation of, 4,
 7, 35
rewards and titles
 received by, 22,
 57–58, 61, 82,
 94–95, 97–98
in Spain, 15–27,
 36, 56–58, *57,*
 70–73, 80–85,
 94–96

Columbus, Christopher, *cont'd.*
will of, 73
Columbus, Diego, 22, 98–99
birth of, 7
in Spain, 15, 16, 54, 62, 81, 99
Columbus, Domenico, 2
Columbus, Ferdinand, 20, 22, 53–54, 62, 81, 99
father's death and, 96, 97
on fourth voyage, 86, 88
Columbus, Giacomo, 2, 61, 68
in Isabela, 66–67, 68
in Santo Domingo, 80
Columbus, Luis, 99
Columbus, Susanna, 2
Correo (La Gorda), 73, 80
Cosa, Juan de la, 25, 49–50, 61
cross-staff, *32*
Cuba, 45–46, 60, 67, 75, 97

D'Albertis, Enrico, *29*
Dias, Bartholomew, 20, 85
Dominican Republic, 45, 46

earth, size and shape of, 8–10, *9*

East Indies, 3, 7–9, 36, 40, 58, 67, 71
Marco Polo and, 12–14
Enriquez de Arana, Beatrice, 20
Enterprise of the Indies, 14–27
financing of, 15, 18–19, 22–23
preparations for, 22–27
Spanish commissions on, 21, 22
equator, 3, 7, 8, 72, 74, 101
Escobedo, Rodrigo de, 39, 51
Esdras, 9, 75
exploration, 1, 5, 21
rights to, 3–4

Ferdinand, King of Spain, 17–19, *18, 26*, 33, 43, 97–98
Columbus helped by, 22–23
Columbus's returns and, 57–58, 94–95
fourth voyage and, 84, 85, 94–95
second voyage and, 59, 70 .
third voyage and, 71–73, 75, 78, 79, 81–82
Fernandina, 43–44
Fieschi, Bartholomew, 91–92, 96

first voyage, 22–58
debate over landing site of, 40–41
false distance chart in, 31, 34–35
false landfalls in, 35, 36
fort built in, 52
journal of, 27, 31, 32, 35, 41–42, 48, 53, 54
land explorations in, 39–48
land sighted in, 37–38
map of, 30
mutiny threat in, 33, 34, 36
recruitment and outfitting for, 23–27
return journey in, 52–56
Florida, 61, 67
food, 28, 33, 45, 63, 66, 70, 73, 100
fourth voyage, 84–95
caravels for, 86
dangers of, 85, 87–93
map of, 87
France, 71, 72, 97

Gama, Vasco da, 85
Genoa, 1–3, 6, 14, 23
globe, Martin Behaim, *9*
gold, 3, 6, 12, 22, 56, 64, 65, 89, 100, 102
Columbus's search for, 43–48, 51

in Hispaniola, 68, 69
Gomera, 29, 62
Granada, 18, 21–22
Grand Canary, 28–30
Guacanagarí, Chief, 48, 50–51, 52, 64
Guadeloupe, 62–63
Guanahaní, 39–43
Gulf of Paria, 75–76, 78
Gutiérrez, Pedro, 37

Haiti, 45, 46, 49
hammocks, 43, *44*
Henry the Navigator, Prince, 5, 6
Hispaniola, 59, 62, 72–73, 74, 82, 90, 98–99
Balboa in, 101–102
Columbus in, 46–52, *47,* 64–70, 77–80, 86–88
Méndez's journey to, 91–93
Hojeda, Alonso de, 65–66, 78, 81, 82, 100

India (Santa Cruz), 70, 73
Indians, 37, 40–48, 90
captive, 46, 56–57, 59, 63, 66, 68, 69–70
converting of, 42, 48, 59, 61, 68
Europeans' conflicts with, 53, 64, 66,

Indians, cont'd.
68, 69–70
hammocks used by, 43, 44
massacres by, 64, 89
as slaves, 68, 70, 78, 103
suicides of, 68, 69
Inquisition, Spanish, 17–18, 19, 27
Isabela, 65–69, 78
Isabella, Queen of Portugal, 71, 82
Isabella, Queen of Spain, 17, 18, 26, 33, 44
Columbus helped by, 19–23, 81–82
Columbus's returns and, 57–58, 70, 94
death of, 94
fourth voyage and, 84, 85, 94
second voyage and, 59, 70
third voyage and, 71–73, 75, 78, 79, 81–82
Isthmus of Panama, 89, 102
Italy, Renaissance in, 21

Jamaica, 67, 90–93
Japan, see Cipangu
Jews, 5
Inquisition and, 17–18, 27

John II, King of Portugal, 5, 15, 16, 56
Juan, Don, 61, 71, 82
Juana, Doña, 71, 94

Kublai Khan, 12, 45

La Castilla (Vaqueños), 73
La Gallega, 61, 86, 89
La Gorda (Correo), 73, 80
La Navidad, 52, 62–65
La Rábida, 16, 17
Las Casas, Bartholomew de, 10–11, 61, 73, 96
Indians defended by, 82, 83, 84, 103–104
"Libretto," 95
Lisbon, 5, 6

Madeira, 5, 7
Magellan, Ferdinand, 102–103
maps, mapmaking, 5, 6, 100, 101, 104
of Columbus's voyages, 30, 60, 72, 87
round earth and, 8, 9
maravedis, 36–37
Margarit, Mosén Pedro, 68
Mariagalante (Santa María), 61, 62

Martinez-Hidalgo, José, 24
Méndez, Diego, 86, 89, 91–94, 96
Michele da Cuneo, Savonese, 61, 70, 86–87
Moors, see Muslims
Muslims, 5
in Spain, 17, 18, 21, 22
Turks, 3, 4
mutiny, 33, 34, 36, 68, 102

navigation, 2, 4, 7, 42
methods of, 31–32, 32
Niña, 26, 28–29, 37, 38, 46, 73
as caravel, 23
model of, 29
name of, 24
Santa María
shipwreck and, 50, 51
on second voyage, 61, 67, 70
in storm, 53–54

Ovando, Nicolás de, 82, 86, 87–88, 93

Pacific Ocean, 89, 101–102
Palos, 15, 23–27, 26
Panama, Isthmus of, 89, 102
Paria, Gulf of, 75–76, 78

pearls, 76, 76, 78, 102
Perestrello y Moniz, Felipa, 7, 15
Pinta, 23, 24, 26, 37, 38, 44
disappearances of, 46, 51–54
model of, 29
repair of, 28–29
sighting of, 53
Pinzón, Martín Alonso, 24–25, 25, 35, 36, 46
Columbus's distrust of, 24–25, 52, 53, 56
death of, 56
Pinzón, Vicente Yañez, 24–25, 25, 35, 82
Polo, Marco, 12–14, 13, 43, 45, 60
Ponce de León, Juan, 61
Porras, Diego de, 86, 92
Porras, Francisco de, 86, 92
Portugal, 3, 5–7, 84, 85
Columbus in, 5–7, 15, 36, 56
Columbus's men seized by, 54, 56
explorations of, 3, 15, 20
Spain's rivalry with, 58
territorial rights of, 3, 58
Puerto Rico, 61, 63

rafts, *42*
rebellions, 77–78, 92
  see also mutiny
Rodríguez de Fonseca,
  Don Juan, 61
Roldán, Francisco, 77–
  78, 81, 88

sailors:
  fears of, 30–31, 34,
    35
  recruitment of, 25–
    27
  routines of, 32–33
Sánchez, Rodrigo, 37,
  39
San Juan, 67
Sanlúcar de
  Barrameda, 74,
  94
San Salvador, 39–43
Santa Clara (formerly
  Niña), 61, 67
Santa Cruz (*India*), 70,
  73
Santa Fé, 21–22, 94
Santa Gloria, 90–94
Santa María, 23–25,
  28, 34–38, 86
  model of, *24*
  shipwreck of, 49–
    51
Santa María
  (*Mariagalante*), 61
Santa Maria de Belén
  (Bethlehem),
  89

Santa María de Guiá, 73
Santa María de la
  Concepción, 43
Santángel, Luis de, 22,
  23
Santiago de Palos
  (*Bermuda*), 86,
  90
Santo Domingo, 74,
  76–78, 90, 97
  Bobadilla in, 79–80
  rebellion in, 77–78
San Tomás (fort), 66,
  68
Sargasso Sea, 35, 53
second voyage, 59–70
  crew for, 61
  European-Indian
    conflicts and, 64,
    66, 68, 69–70
  instructions for,
    59–60
  map of, 60
  mutiny in, 68
  secrecy of route on,
    62
  settlement attempts
    in, 65–69
ships:
  naming of, 23–24
  speed of, 31–32
Sierra Leone, 74
silver, 12, 22, 100
slaves, 6, 68, 70, 78,
  103
South America, 75,
  102–103

Spain:
  Columbus in, 15–
    27, 36, 56–58,
    57, 70–73, 80–
    85, 94–96
  15th century (map),
    20
  Inquisition in, 17–
    18, *19, 27*
  Portugal's rivalry
    with, 58
  royal marriages in,
    71
  territorial rights of,
    3–4, 58
Strait of Magellan, 103

Tainos, 48, 50–52,
  64–66, 68–70,
  91–93
Talavera, Hernando de,
  21
Talavera Commission,
  21
Terreros, Pedro de, 61,
  86
third voyage, 71–84
  lands explored
    during, 74–76
  map of, 72
  recruitment for,
    72–73
  return journey in,
    80
  route in, 72, 74
Torres, Antonio de,
  61, 81

Torres, Luis de, 42, 51
Toscanelli, Paolo dal
  Pozzo (Paul the
  Physician), 10–
  11
  chart of, 10, *10*
trade, 60, 91, 100
  maritime, 2–3
  Portuguese-African,
    5–6
Triana, Rodrigo de, 37
Trinidad, 74–75
Tristán, Diego, 61, 86,
  89

Valladolid, 94, 96
Vaqueños (*La Castilla*),
  73
Venezuela, 75
Venice, 2–3
  Marco Polo in, 12,
    13, 14
Vespucci, Amerigo, *79,*
  100–101
Victoria, 103
Vikings, 99
Vizcaína, 86

Waldseemüller,
  Martin, 101, *104*
West Indies, 40
winds, 7, 29, 65, 69,
  74
  trade, 31, 34, 35,
    52

Xaraguá, 77